P

C000135839

"Masterly and rich... Highly recommended." — *Library Journal* (**Starred Review**)

"A surprisingly engrossing erotic thriller... Reisz writes sadomasochistic scenes that are charged with love and care alongside the sex and suffering, and Kingsley is an engaging hero..." — *The New York Times Book Review*

"Fantastic... The characters are strong, and there is enough mystery that the twists feel well earned... Highly recommended to both new readers and those who are already familiar with Kingsley's world." — *Publishers Weekly* (**Starred Review**)

"Feminists are once again making a stand in the world and the timing seems quite perfect as this novel is an intriguing look into the world of a strong, sadistic and mysterious woman." — **Kelsey's Korner Blog**

"Simply stunning. It's bold, kinky, romantic, and I highly recommend it." — **Read All the Romance**

THE RETURN

MORE ORIGINAL SINNERS

Novels

THE SIREN (Book #1) • THE ANGEL (Book #2)

THE PRINCE (Book #3) • THE MISTRESS (Book #4)

THE SAINT (Book #5) 8 THE KING (Book #6)

THE VIRGIN (Book #7) • THE QUEEN (Book #8)

THE PRIEST (Book #9)

THE CHATEAU (Standalone)

PICTURE PERFECT COWBOY (Standalone)

Novellas and Collections

THE CONFESSIONS

THE GIFT (previously published as SEVEN DAY LOAN)

IMMERSED IN PLEASURE

THE LAST GOOD KNIGHT (PARTS I—V)

LITTLE RED RIDING CROP • MICHAEL'S WINGS

MISCHIEF • THE MISTRESS FILES

SOMETHING NICE • SUBMIT TO DESIRE

WINTER TALES

TIFFANY REISZ

The Return

8TH CIRCLE PRESS
LOUISVILLE, KY

The Return

Copyright © 2018, 2020 Tiffany Reisz

The Return was previously published as "The Story of Ø" in the limited-edition, signed-and-numbered hardcover edition of Tiffany Reisz's *The Chateau*.

Mass-market Paperback ISBN: 978-1-949769-15-9

Also available as an eBook.

Cover design by Andrew Shaffer. Elements used under license from Shutterstock.com.

www.8thcirclepress.com

First Edition

The Return is a sequel novella to the Original Sinners novel *The Chateau.*

It was previously published under the title "The Story of Ø" in the limited-edition, signed-and-numbered hardcover edition of *The Chateau.*

CHAPTER ONE

When Kingsley had been whipped within an inch of his life, and the sex after had nearly taken the other inch, he lay across Søren's stomach, ready to greet Death with a smile.

"Move," Søren ordered.

"I can't. You killed me."

Kingsley's head rose and fell like driftwood on an ocean wave with the force of Søren's sigh.

"Why is it always my stomach?" Søren asked. His tone was rhetorical...*and* disgusted. "There are organs in there. Delicate organs. Namely the diaphragm which controls breathing. Your head on my diaphragm makes it more than slightly difficult to breathe."

"You have a sexy stomach. Not my fault." Kingsley turned his head and kissed said sexy stomach which inspired another disgusted, yet resigned, sigh on Søren's part. Another ocean wave. An icy winter ocean.

"Eleanor at least has the common decency to

wallow around on my chest where there is a ribcage to keep me from dying of slow suffocation. You have to lay ten pounds of French cranium onto my stomach. Where's a guillotine when I need it?"

"Decapitation is my hard limit."

"So he *finally* finds a hard limit," Søren said. "Only took a few decades."

Smiling, Kingsley kissed Søren's stomach again...kissed that pale smooth hard stomach and the firm elegant curve of ribcage...and his sternum, hard as iron, and up and down the center of his chest and then, finally, one kiss over the heart, if there was a heart in there. Sometimes Kingsley still wondered...

But Kingsley did feel the slow steady thrum of something heart-like in there. After the sustained, back-lacerating whipping Kingsley had just endured, he had a feeling it was a clock there. A ticking clock attached to a brick of C-4 explosives.

"Are you about to blow?" Kingsley asked.

"You? Or in general?"

"Me."

"Try asking nicely for once in your heathen life."

"Will you please blow me, Sir?"

"Absolutely not."

"I asked nicely."

"I told you to *try* asking nicely. I never promised it would work."

"Bastard."

"You came twice. Don't be so greedy."

Kingsley was greedy though. He'd had a perfect day and when that wasn't enough, he'd demanded a perfect night as well. And it had been a perfect day. They lived in New Orleans now, all of them. Kingsley, his lover Juliette, their daughter Céleste. Søren, too, and his lover Nora. They'd come to give Céleste a better, happier childhood than they could have given her in Manhattan. And they had. Earlier that day, he and Juliette had taken Céleste to the nature reserve where she'd marveled at the playing otters and lumbering alligators, giggled madly at the flittering blue butterflies and flat-footed penguins.

A perfect day. Strangers complimented Kingsley on his beautiful family, on Céleste's sweet temper and infectious laugh. Another family with a daughter of about twelve asked Kingsley to take their photograph in front of the flamingos. And he had as if he were a normal husband and father and not one of the more notorious men in the BDSM communities of New York and New Orleans.

Happiness had swollen in his chest like a red balloon, about to burst. Home again that afternoon, he put Céleste down for her nap, and found Juliette in the kitchen, baking bread for their dinner.

"I think today was one of the best days of my life," Kingsley told her as he held her from behind, hands on her stomach, lips at her ear. "Top ten, at least. Who knew being vanilla could be so fun?"

"Céleste wants a girls night tonight so we can do our hair and nails. You should call Søren."

"Are you trying to get rid of me?" Kingsley had teased her, though he'd had the thought himself.

"I'm trying to save you from yourself before you really do turn vanilla," she said. "If you buy a grill and start wearing boat shoes, *mon roi et mon amour,* I will leave you and never look back."

"What's wrong with boat shoes?" Kingsley asked.

She swatted him with a spatula.

"Call Søren right now."

So Kingsley had called Søren. It required humbling himself. Well, whoring himself really, which he was more than willing to do. But it had been such a good day and every gambler knew to ride a hot hand. And had anyone ever said they were "too happy"? Was there such a thing?

Søren had made it more difficult, of course.

"It's a school night," Søren said when Kingsley had asked to see him.

So Kingsley had replied, "School me, then."

"Eight o'clock. Your apartment."

Eight o'clock came.

And so had Kingsley.

Twice.

Kingsley's "apartment" didn't really deserve

that name. It wasn't much more than a grand bedroom suite with a bathroom on the second floor of the house he'd purchased for the sole purpose of building a friendly little BDSM society in town. And because he did not lack a sense of irony or sense of history, his new place was in the French Quarter.

The Marquis Club was intimate, elegant, and exclusive—so very exclusive most people in New Orleans wouldn't know it existed even if they tried looking for such a place, which is exactly how Kingsley wanted it.

As much as he'd loved The 8th Circle in New York, he vastly preferred The Marquis Club. A double gallery historic home with six bedrooms —now converted to dungeons—it had once served as a New Orleans brothel. The back balconies overlooked a courtyard shielded by a high wall for private parties. And downstairs one would find an exquisitely-appointed reception room where the well-heeled perverts of Louisiana came to mingle before slipping off to a private playroom. In a gilded frame on a wall in that reception room hung a portrait of Donatien Alphonse François, AKA the Marquis de Sade.

Even now as he dozed on his lover's stomach, Kingsley could hear the murmur of voices below them in the drawing room and the gentle din of the jazz trio that played at The Marquis Club every Friday and Saturday night. Juliette's idea...make The Marquis Club appear to be nothing more than another jazz club. To which the infamous dominatrix Mistress Nora had to add, "Brilliant— hide your jizz club inside your jazz club."

Kingsley hadn't laughed but only because he was pissed he hadn't thought of the joke first.

"Are you asleep?" Kingsley asked Søren when several minutes of silence had passed.

Kingsley had simply been marinating in his good fortune. God only knew what went on in Søren's mind when quietly ruminating.

"Awake," Søren said. "Not easy to sleep when I have a human skull compressing my lungs."

Kingsley lifted his head from Søren's stomach.

"Thank God." Søren took a deep melodramatic breath.

"Does it really hurt that much?"

"Yes."

"Good."

Søren, without warning, lightly chopped Kingsley in the diaphragm with the side of his hand.

Two minutes later Kingsley took a deep breath for the first time in two minutes.

"I don't know what's more humiliating," Kingsley said as he took another breath. "That I didn't see that coming or that I enjoyed it."

"You are the whore of whores. Whores who have spent the past twenty years on their backs look at you and say, 'Have some dignity, man, for God's sake. You're making us all look bad.'"

Kingsley laughed though it hurt. Or perhaps...because it hurt.

"The sadist of sadists has no room to talk. Even my Madame would tell you, 'Pace yourself, boy. No use beating a dead whore.'"

Kingsley expected a reaction to that. One of his better plays on words that evening. A laugh? A smile? Søren didn't even blink.

Unforgivably rude.

Søren left the bed and walked naked across the floor to the chair that held his clothes. He wore his naked body like other men wore tailored Armani suits, with the casual confidence of someone who knew he was the best-dressed man in the room.

Kingsley forgave Søren. Ah, puns were the lowest form of humor.

He watched his lover dress with nearly the same pleasure he'd watched him undress. The flex of long legs and steely quads, the taut tensing of biceps, the stretch and flash of back muscle...best show in town.

Now dressed apart from socks and shoes, Søren returned to the bed. He stood over Kingsley who lay on his back, still naked, hands clasped behind his head.

"Speaking of Madame," Søren said. "I have to tell you something."

"What?" Kingsley instantly sat up.

"I don't know if you'll want to know this, but I

admit I couldn't help myself. Curiosity got the better of me," Søren said.

"What the hell are you talking about?"

Søren took a folded sheet of paper from the pocket of his black jeans and held it out to Kingsley who only stared at it.

"I believe I found your château."

CHAPTER TWO

Kingsley and Søren flew into Charles de Gaulle Airport where they picked up their car—a sleek black Peugeot RCZ—for their long drive to the château.

The decision to go had been an easy one for Kingsley. He'd done the math. Madame, if she were still alive, would be seventy-four now. If he wanted to see her again, he shouldn't wait. He hadn't even realized he'd wanted to see her or the château again until Søren had presented him with the possibility.

Although the decision had been immediate, they'd had to delay the trip for two weeks.

"I'll go with you," Søren had said the night of his bombshell revelation that he'd found Madame's address. "If you can wait until my Spring Break."

Kingsley recalled shaking his head, too bemused to laugh.

"Only you would want to visit an elderly sadist on your Spring Break."

"Would you prefer Miami Beach?"

Kingsley would not. He was fifty and though he barely passed for forty and still turned the heads of women of all ages, the only thing Kingsley ever wanted a college girl for these days was as a babysitter for Céleste.

And so the trip was planned and here they were, driving into the Aube region of France to a small village near Troyes.

Troyes, where according to the records of the Catholic Church in France, an eighteen-year-old girl named Alice Olympia de Lacy married Captain Edouard Masson in the winter of 1959.

The marriage certificate included the address for the Masson family château.

"Do I want to know how many favors you called in to find the address?" Kingsley asked as they sped along the autoroute where, twenty-six years ago, Kingsley had been taken blindfolded in a burgundy car, his head on Madame's thigh.

"Only one." Søren turned his head from the passenger window. "I know the priest who has been working for years to digitize parish records before all the old registers crumble to dust. Took him a month but he found it."

"What do you owe him?"

"*You* owe him a week's vacation in Nice at a five-star resort with an ocean view."

"Done," Kingsley said.

"You could have found the address yourself," Søren reminded him.

"I could. I didn't."

"Why not?"

"I don't know," Kingsley admitted. "Like I told you last winter, it didn't feel real. Not until I told you about it. After...I thought about looking but knew I wouldn't go back. Not alone."

"You aren't alone."

Kingsley smiled to himself. Were there any three words more beautiful than those? *You aren't alone?*

"I can't believe I'll see the place again tonight." Kingsley shook his head.

"Caveat—all I have is the address. If the documents were forged or altered, if Madame is dead, if she's moved..."

"It's fine," Kingsley said. "Whatever happens, it's fine."

"Are you certain?"

"I'm in France with you. Do you have any idea how long I've wanted this?"

"A long time?"

"I used to dream about it," Kingsley confessed. "Back in school. You and me, running away to live in France together. Stupid teenage fantasies." He almost blushed.

"You never asked me to run away with you," Søren said.

"I knew you would have said no. Wouldn't you?"

Søren didn't answer. Not out of sadism, it seemed, but because he saw something.

"There." Søren pointed out his window. Kingsley brought the car to a sudden stop. He peered through the dark and saw a break in the forest, a long winding drive, the outline of an elaborate iron gate, and behind it, a château.

"That's it," Kingsley said, the words unnecessary. For no other house would he have slammed on the brakes.

His heart leapt into his throat. He turned the engine off and got out of the car. For a moment he stared but then walked to the edge of the drive and stood there. There, but barely there. One step forward, and he'd be on the property of the château. One step only. Søren came and stood at his side.

"That's where I chose you," Kingsley said.

"You chose me over Madame, a woman you barely knew."

"I chose you over everything else I ever wanted, even children. I chose you when I hadn't seen or heard from you in seven years."

"Why did you do that again?"

"Fuck, I have no idea."

They both laughed, the tension broken. The Kingsley noticed something.

"Look." He pointed at a window, glowing red from inside. "That's Madame's playroom. She has to be alive, right?"

It was then that Kingsley realized exactly why

he'd come back after twenty-six years and why he'd waited two weeks for Søren to accompany him on this pilgrimage.

"I can't wait to introduce you to her," Kingsley said.

"You think she'll approve of me?"

"I hope not."

"Shall we?" Søren asked.

"We came all this way. Might as well. But..." Kingsley turned around and glanced at the car. "Let's leave the car here."

"In case we have to make a run for it?" Søren asked.

"You never know with sadists. They're fucking crazy," Kingsley said. Søren slapped him on the back of the head.

"Come on, whore. It's getting late."

Søren strode ahead through the iron gate, which was unlocked and open wide enough to admit foot traffic. Kingsley took a deep breath then caught up with Søren. As they neared the château, Kingsley felt a wave of regret. Was this a stupid idea, coming here? Probably. He could be at home right now, in bed with his Jules. He imagined her wrists tied to the headboard and her long lovely dark legs wrapped around his hips as he fucked her insensate.

That made him feel a little better. But really...what did he want from this trip? Would he get anything out of this other than awkward chit-chat, if that? Was this all a mistake?

Kingsley might have returned to the car had he been alone. But he couldn't humiliate himself in front of Søren by chickening out. Instead he matched Søren's long strides and carried on toward the grand house with the riverstone facade.

They reached the door and Kingsley paused, not quite ready to ring the bell.

"I never know how to dress for these occasions," Kingsley said. He'd worn black trousers, a white shirt, collar open, and a black jacket. Søren wore a gray suit, no tie, to look "inconspicuous," he'd said. He was six-foot-four, a Nordic god with steel-gray eyes that could best a hawk in a staring contest.

Inconspicuous he was not.

"Do I look okay?" Kingsley asked. He straightened his jacket, smoothed his shirt.

"You look, as Eleanor would say, stupid handsome. Now ring the bell."

Kingsley took a steadying breath. "No. Kiss me first."

Søren made a disgusted face. "Do I have to?"

"What if she kills us? Last chance for a kiss goodbye."

"She won't kill both of us."

"You don't think?"

Søren glanced over his shoulder in the general direction of the gate—their escape route.

"I can outrun you," Søren said.

Kingsley sighed heavily. "I could be grilling in boat shoes right now." He reached for the bell.

Before Kingsley could hit the button, Søren grasped him by the back of the neck for a kiss, a hard one. Kingsley's mouth was forced open. Sparks sparked when their tongues touched. Even more and even better, was the pressure of Søren's fingers digging into Kingsley's skin, right at the top of his spine, immobilizing him like a kitten dangling from his mother's teeth. Kingsley went limp against Søren, limp but for one part of him that was decidedly not limp.

Limp and hard, the perfect slave to a perfect sadist. Then Søren broke the kiss and slapped his cheek.

"Now ring the doorbell before your erection does it for you," Søren said.

"Fine." Before Kingsley's finger touched the button, Søren spoke softly.

"I won't let her hurt you again," he said. "That's my job."

"What if she hurts you?" A real possibility. They were walking into the lion's den. But, Kingsley reminded himself, he would be fine. He had a wolf with him.

"Nothing hurts when I'm with you."

Kingsley rang the bell.

CHAPTER THREE

At first, nothing happened. The house echoed with only silence.

Then Kingsley heard footsteps approaching the door, soft and quick, female footsteps in high heels.

The door opened to reveal a beautiful woman who said simply, "Yes? Hello?"

She had long straight chocolate-brown hair, dark eyes, olive skin, and a tiny beauty mark on her chin.

"Hello, Colette," Kingsley said. "And hello, Georges."

He had her at a disadvantage. He'd half-expected to see Colette on this trip. She'd likely imagined she'd never see him again as long as she lived. But though so much time had passed, he knew she recognized him. She must have. Only explanation for why she slammed the door in his face.

At least she tried to slam the door.

Before the door could close all the way, Søren stopped it with his hand.

Kingsley couldn't decide what was more surprising—Colette's fearful reaction or Søren's aggressive move to stop the door from shutting them out.

"He's not here to hurt anyone," Søren said in his flawless French.

Colette's wide eyes finally seemed to take in Søren's presence.

"Are you certain, *Monsieur*?" she asked.

"I promise," Kingsley said. "I came only to see Madame and pay my respects to her."

Colette hesitated, saying nothing but studying his face intently.

"You were told never to return," Colette said.

"I know. But if there's a chance I could speak with her, if only for a moment... It's been twenty-six years. At least ask her before you send us away. And, as you see, I'm unarmed."

He opened his jacket to show he carried no weapons.

"And your friend?" She lifted her chin in Søren's general direction. She already seemed to have taken a dislike to Søren. Kingsley didn't really blame her.

"I'm a pacifist," Søren said.

Colette snorted in derision. "What are you? A Buddhist monk?"

"Close enough," Søren said. His eyes were hard, cruel. He met Colette like an old enemy.

Or a jealous boyfriend.

Kingsley was enjoying this immensely.

"I don't like him," Colette said to Kingsley.

Kingsley replied, "Your taste in men is impeccable, as always."

Søren's eyebrow cocked a millimeter or two. And Colette...she smiled. A little. A very little. *Un petit peu.*

Then she stepped back and let them into the château.

Søren went inside first. As master or shield, Kingsley couldn't say, but he appreciated it either way. Kingsley entered after him and the very second he did, he knew for certain Madame was still alive.

How? He could smell her perfume in the air. Lavender water, like his mother used to wear.

The scent comforted him. Not much could have changed if Madame were still alive and Colette here.

Kingsley followed Søren and Colette down a hall to the drawing room where Madame had taken him the first night and the last day.

She said nothing but Kingsley wanted her talking again. He had a thousand questions but knew Frenchwomen did not respond well to being interrogated.

"Seems so quiet," Kingsley said. "Has everyone left?"

"We have a second house now," she said. "In Troyes. So many children and grandchildren, the village school couldn't handle all of them. We spend the week in Troyes and the weekends and holidays here. But Madame prefers it here. So do I. Good memories." She smiled, a little shyly, and Kingsley had to return the smile.

"You're more beautiful now than you were then," Kingsley said as she opened the door to the drawing room. "And you were stunning then."

A compliment, yes, but not empty flattery. She was still slim and lovely. She wore tight jeans, a crisp white blouse, red high heels and a matching red scarf in her hair. The math said she was forty-four but his eyes refused to believe it. If he'd passed her on the street and they'd been strangers, he would have guessed she was thirty-five.

"Too kind," she said, her tone dismissive though he thought he glimpsed a gleam of pleasure in her eyes. "You look well, too. But you should have worn a tuxedo."

"Like I wore when we got married?" he asked. She smiled broadly now.

"*Married,*" she repeated, rolling her eyes and turning the word into a joke. That was how he felt about marriage, too.

"I'm touched you even remember me," Kingsley said.

"A girl never forgets her first." Colette touched him lightly on the chest, over his heart. Søren cleared his throat. Colette pulled her hand away as if she'd been scalded.

Or scolded.

"Wait here, please," she said.

She left them alone in the drawing room. Søren stood at the fireplace where a low fire smoldered. Kingsley wandered the room, too nervous to stand still.

"You feeling a little possessive, *mon ami*?" Kingsley asked, hands in his trouser pockets, playing casual.

"She faked a pregnancy to torture you." Søren turned and rested his back against the mantel. "I won't allow her to pretend that didn't happen."

"I like this side of you." Kingsley shook his finger at Søren. "I enjoy watching you be vicious to other people almost as much as I enjoy it when you're vicious to me."

"Good. I intend to continue to be vicious until we're gone."

"Maybe I won't leave?" Kingsley couldn't help but push his luck a little. "Maybe they'll make me an even better offer than last time."

"I will carry you out if I must, and if I don't, Juliette will."

He smiled at the mere thought of Søren and Juliette teaming up to bodily remove him from this place. As if he'd ever leave either of them—not for all the kink, sex, money, and châteaux in the wide world.

Kingsley continued to pace the room. It looked as it had in his memories—beautifully furnished with antiques, though now black and white photographs in black frames hung on the walls where paintings once had. Kingsley recognized Polly in one photograph, dressed in an evening gown with one of the men of the household on her arm. One fabulous photograph showcased all the women of the house arrayed like a family photo, all of them in matching gowns of white.

"Søren, come look." Kingsley pointed at series of photographs hung in a line on the wall. Søren walked over and leaned past Kingsley's shoulder to study them.

"Who is it?"

"Jacques, the baby. Not a baby anymore." Kingsley watched Jacques age in the photographs from an infant to a toddler, to a school-aged boy with crooked front teeth, to a handsome smiling teenager with a rakish grin. In the last photograph he stood in front of a shining new VW, his arm around Madame's waist. Madame looked like a doting grandmother who'd given a car to her grandson on his graduation day.

"He's twenty-five, twenty-six now. Nico's age," Kingsley said. "I wanted children so badly, and had no idea I had a son already."

Kingsley had made this same lament before. Søren squeezed Kingsley's shoulder in sympathy.

But Søren's attention was taken by another photograph. Kingsley moved over and saw Søren gazing at a picture of Colette with two young women on either side of her. They all three sat on a divan in this very room and smiled at the camera. They were beauties, all of them.

Colette returned to the drawing room just then. It was clear she knew what photograph they were studying and what they all were thinking.

She walked over to them and pointed at the girl on her right who wore a ruffled sundress.

"Salome," she said. "She's nineteen. Heloise." She pointed at the girl on her left who held a bouquet of violets in her hand. "She's twenty-two. My only children, if you were wondering."

"I was," Søren said. Colette stiffened, feeling the insult. "Heloise... she who caused her tutor Abelard to be exiled and castrated. Salome, who demanded and received John the Baptist's head on a platter. Interesting choice of names for your daughters."

"I don't hate men, *Monsieur*."

"Sheer coincidence then that your daughters are named for women who destroyed men?" Søren asked.

"I didn't say that." Colette smiled wickedly. "I enjoy hurting men. But I don't hate them. You seem to hate strong women, however."

Kingsley snorted. He couldn't help it. It just came out. Colette looked at him as if he'd lost his mind.

"Sorry," Kingsley said.

"As Kingsley's so very attractive snorting attests," Søren continued, "I don't dislike strong women at all. I happen to love one, as a matter of fact. My dislike of you, I assure you, is purely personal."

"I won't apologize for what we did to him." Colette lifted her chin again, shameless, fearless, delicious. "He was warned. Not our fault he was too stupid to listen to Madame."

"You played your part," Søren said. "You didn't have to, did you?"

"I was only eighteen. I did as I was told," she said, her eyes blazing with pure indignation.

"Ah, so you're her submissive then, not a dominant. Now I understand," Søren said. "All's forgiven."

God, Kingsley had never wanted popcorn more in his life. He was in absolute Heaven. Was this a new kink of his? Watching Søren be unconscionably bitchy to his former lovers? This was so much hotter than a whipping.

"Madame," Colette said, as she pointedly turned her back to Søren, "is very ill. Very, very ill."

"I'm sorry," Kingsley said. "Truly."

"But she is awake, and she will see you for a few minutes."

"I won't keep her long." Kingsley knew it would be hard to see her so old and fragile but he'd come this far.

"You misunderstand." Colette pursed her lovely lips and both her hands tightened into fists. "She does not want to see you, Kingsley. I was speaking to him."

"Him?" Kingsley pointed at Søren. "Why him and not me? She doesn't even know him."

"Because she's already played with you," Søren said. He sounded irritated but not particularly surprised. "I am, as they say, fresh meat."

"*Exactement*," Colette said. "You wait here."

She waved her hand as a queen would summon a lowly servant. Søren followed her from the room, but on the way out, he winked at Kingsley.

Alone in the room, Kingsley spoke one word —in English, since there was no precise French equivalent.

"Mother*fucker*."

CHAPTER FOUR

K ingsley seethed. He'd come all this
way...twenty-six years...crossed an ocean...
He even got his hair cut...

And Madame would only see Søren?

And he had to wait here like a child while the
sadistic love of his life had an intimate tête-à-tête
with the most remorseless mind-fucker Kingsley
had ever known? Apart from Søren, of course.

Who did they think he was? A suburban father with a grill, boat shoes, and a Ford Explorer?
He was Kingsley-Fucking-Edge and there were
grown men who still pissed themselves when
they heard his name whispered in their
nightmares.

It had been a long time but Kingsley was a
former spy and had a spy's memory for layouts
and escape routes. He took off his jacket, opened
the sash on the window behind the sofa, and
slipped out of the house, shutting the window be-

hind him. No screens to contend with as summer was still two months away.

He needed and found a rainspout with iron bars that strapped it to the stonework. It was nothing to shimmy up the spout like a ladder and jump onto the balcony. And the balcony, as he remembered, ran the entire length of the second story. He walked it until he found an unlocked door, slipped into a darkened room and only when he reached the hallway door did he recall what room this had once been—Jacques's nursery.

Kingsley glanced around, seeing in his mind's eye the rocking chair, the bassinet, the little nightlight in the shape of a lamb. It was in this room where he'd held Jacques against his bare chest while Madame had interrogated him about Søren. That night had been the first night Kingsley had spoken of him in seven years.

No time for reminiscing. The hall was clear. Kingsley ran for it.

He reached the end of the wing and two doors greeted him. On the left, Madame's bedroom. On the right, the room that had once been her husband's before she kicked the man out of the house, burned their bed to spite him, and turned his room into her dungeon.

Leaning in, Kingsley heard the murmur of Colette's voice coming through the door on his right. Why would Madame, a very ill 74-year-old woman, be in her playroom and not her bedroom? Kingsley didn't have time to wonder about it. He slipped into Madame's bedroom, the door on the left, and into the Jack and Jill bathroom that connected her room with her husband's old bedroom.

Kingsley crept to the bathroom door and listened, ears perked as he heard Colette speaking sharply.

"You can't mean that," Colette said. "You don't even know him. I would never leave you with a stranger. Especially this stranger."

Ah, so Madame wanted to be left alone with Søren and Colette disapproved.

Søren, wisely, kept his mouth shut and let the women argue it out.

"But I do, don't I?" Madame's voice was soft and tremulous. Kingsley winced to hear Madame sounding so faded.

"Deep calls unto deep," Søren said.

Kingsley's brow furrowed. Where had he heard that before? Deep calls unto deep? Back in school. Had to be a Psalm. That's right. Some Psalm. Intuitively he understood what it meant. *Deep calls unto deep.* Søren was saying he and Madame were, deep down, the very same.

"Go, child. Off with you. I'll be fine."

Kingsley pictured Madame waving a weak hand to shoo Colette from the room.

"Fine," Colette said. "If you want to be insane, be insane. I want no part of this. If they kill you and steal the silver, it's not my fault."

Colette left with a huff and a slam of the door.

God, Kingsley did love a woman with a French temper.

But thank fuck he didn't end up with her. Juliette didn't have a temper. She didn't need one. She only had to look at him, expressionless, and Kingsley went out and bought her six dozen roses, orchids, and jewelry.

Now Søren and Madame were alone.

Plus, one eavesdropper.

"Forgive her," Madame said. "She hides her fear behind her anger."

"I may have gotten on her bad side."

"Good," Madame said. "She's spoiled. Always has been. She needs to be told 'no' more often."

"I promise, we aren't here to kill you or steal the silver," Søren said. "Unless it's very good silver."

"I'll be dead soon. Have at it."

Søren laughed softly, politely. "She does seem afraid. I assume Kingsley isn't the first of your old playthings to pay you a visit?"

"Three others have come," she said. "One came back to demand money or he'd reveal my location. Another came back to demand I apologize. The third wanted to kill me."

"He didn't succeed."

"My husband dealt with him."

"Your husband?" Kingsley heard the surprise in Søren's voice, surprise that mirrored his own. "You and your husband reconciled?"

"Finally, yes. Not long after Kingsley left us. He's buried here in his family's plot, as he always wanted."

"I'm sorry for your loss."

"Ah, we had twelve good years before I lost him again. I was hardly more than a child when we married. The girl in me despised him like a child despises a cruel father. But when we came together again, I was a grown woman and then some. The woman's heart in me did find a way to love him, even if the girl could not ever truly forgive him."

She fell silent and took a labored breath.

"But better," she went on, "to love and hate the man on the pillow next to mine than to have no one asleep on the pillow next to me at all. But you know how that is, don't you? Kingsley loved you, hated you, forgave you. And you were once only boys."

"When we met he was a boy. I was a beast. When we met again, I was twenty-nine, and he was twenty-eight. Then I was almost human. Almost."

"Are you human now?"

"For your sake, Madame," he said, "I will pretend to be." His voice held none of the rancor he'd expended on Colette. "Can I get you anything?"

"No, no, I'm fine for a dying woman. Here. Sit close so I can see you. My eyes aren't what they were."

Kingsley heard Søren's footsteps and a chair being lifted and moved. While Kingsley had sound to cover his own sounds, he sunk to the floor and peered through the keyhole into the room.

He saw Madame in a bed. A large bed, big enough for two, with a tufted silk headboard and a dozen thick white satin pillows propping Madame up. She looked so small and thin, with her long white hair in a braid over her shoulder. And yet, still lovely in a way, still striking. Good cheekbones never went out of style.

Søren sat in the club chair he'd moved near her bed.

Madame looked at him and he looked at her. If this turned into a battle of wills, Kingsley knew they might be there for days. But no, Madame was looking at Søren for the same reason everyone did.

"You're as handsome as he said you were," she said. "Søren."

"Thank you, Alice."

"I didn't say you could address me by my first name."

"I didn't say you could address me by mine. In fact, I don't believe I told Colette my name. How did you know it was me?"

"Who else would he bring here? Only you. To gloat, I suppose."

"No." Søren shook his head. "I would not have

allowed him to come if that had been his intention."

"Allowed him? So you are his master?"

"I am."

"So sorry."

Søren smiled. Even Kingsley smiled in his hiding place.

"Why did he come then?" she asked. "To apologize? To ask forgiveness?"

"To pay his respects. You helped him work through a few things, I believe. But he can tell you that."

"And you both came all the way from America to visit me here. I'm touched."

Madame didn't sound very touched.

"Kingsley's grown son Nicholas lives in France. They're spending a day together in Paris this week while I'll be exploring Notre-Dame and Sacrê-Cœur. And a few of Kingsley's parents' things are in storage. He's been meaning for years to come back and see if there's anything worth salvaging. I'm only along for the ride, as they say."

"Don't pretend you weren't curious about me."

"I'm here, aren't I? I could have let Kingsley come alone."

"But you couldn't do that, could you? You say he's not here to gloat, but he does want me to see who he chose over me."

"Perhaps," Søren said.

"Why did he choose you? Your pretty face?" She raised her hand and patted Søren on his cheek. And Søren, shockingly, allowed it.

"You'll have to ask him why." Søren took her hand in his and gently pressed it into the covers.

"I'm done with him. I am asking *you*."

"I won't tell you."

"I'm dying," she said.

"Aren't we all?"

Kingsley laughed again behind his hand.

"Søren," she said again. "Swedish?"

"Danish," he said.

"But you're also Marcus if I remember correctly."

"You do," he said. "You have an impressive memory."

"Where the weaknesses of men are concerned, I have a photographic memory."

"I have no doubt you do," Søren said. "Your husband was a lucky man, wasn't he?"

Kingsley knew she'd been a world-class spy in her younger years as she'd amassed blackmail material galore to force her husband to come to heel. A spy had to listen to conversations while pretending not to listen, had to remember everything while betraying nothing, had to hold secrets in her head until she could write them down. Oh, yes, Kingsley didn't doubt for one second Madame remembered every single thing he'd told her about Søren, banking it in a vault for the day she could spend that knowledge like a child in a candy store.

Seemed Madame still had a sweet tooth.

"How is it that you're both a Marcus and a Søren?"

"That topic is not open for discussion."

"You're not much fun, Søren." She waved her hand, swatting his protestations away like a fly.

"Why should I be? It's cruel of you to refuse to see him. I'm only here for him, not you. I could leave now, spend the rest of the night inside Kingsley, and we'll both have forgotten you exist by morning."

Silence.

Silence except for Kingsley's madly beating heart. He had to cover his mouth with his hand to muffle the shattering breath he took at Søren's words. To hear that...his heart nearly left his body. He'd never felt so owned.

Finally, Madame spoke.

"Deep calls unto deep. I feel like I'm seeing my soul in the mirror. I never thought I had a soul and now here I find out it's a handsome blond. Such a pleasant surprise."

Madame laughed to herself but the laugh quickly turned into a horrific cough that came from deep within her slight body.

The cough finally subsided.

Poor lady. Kingsley hated to think of her in this kind of pain.

"If you need your rest, Madame," Søren said, "I can leave you to it."

"No, no, no, I feel better with you here. It's been a long time since I've played with such a pretty toy."

"You wish to play with me?"

"Of course," she said. "As you wish to play with me. Shall we pick a prize?"

"Kingsley's happiness is my price and my prize."

"Good. Let's play for it then. One hour. You answer every question I ask you and you answer it honestly, and I'll see him, briefly."

"And if I don't want to answer one of these questions?"

"*Adieu.*"

Kingsley pictured Madame raising her hand to wave him goodbye.

"Is this game too rough for you?" Madame taunted.

"I've played it before."

"Shall we play it again?"

"Half an hour," Søren said. Kingsley rolled his eyes. Cheap bastard.

"Forty-five minutes," she countered.

"Forty."

"Forty then. More than enough."

"In the interest of full disclosure," Søren said, "anything I tell you that I haven't told Kingsley...I will tell him as soon as I can. I won't allow you to know more about me than he does."

"In the interest of full disclosure," Madame said, "I don't give a damn what you tell or don't tell Kingsley. Shall we play?"

Søren said nothing and in the long silence Kingsley said a prayer to a God he wasn't certain he believed in.

Play the game. Play the game. God, please let him play the game. I'll start going to Mass with Juliette and Céleste if they play this fucking game.

"Very well," Søren said. "Let's play."

CHAPTER FIVE

"It's 9:14," Søren said. "You have until 9:54. Go."

"Why is your name Marcus *and* Søren?" she asked.

Fuck. Kingsley already knew the answer to this one. What a waste of time.

"I'm a child of rape," Søren said. "My father raped my eighteen-year-old mother when she was working for the family as a nanny for my newborn sister. He was wealthy and powerful and sent my mother away when I was five. I'd shown enough promise by then—I learned to read and play piano very early, among other things that caught his interest. He decided to legitimize me in case he never had any other sons. He gave me his name, Marcus. But I already knew myself by the name my mother had given me—Søren, her father's name. To those I love and who love me, I'm Søren. On my business cards, I'm Marcus. If I had business cards, that is."

Although Kingsley had known this story, it still hurt him to hear it.

"You told Kingsley your real name the first night you had sex, he told me. That meant something to him, that he was the only one who knew your real name. He said that was why he chose you over me, because you would tell him your real name, and I wouldn't."

"I'm sure that isn't the only reason," Søren said.

God, what a bastard. Here was Madame dying and Søren was taunting her. Kingsley had never loved him more in his life.

"It's 9:18," Søren said.

"Are you faithful to Kingsley?"

Kingsley's eyes widened in the dark shadows of the bathroom. Couldn't she asked normal nosy questions like "What do you do for a living?" or "How big is your cock?"

Kingsley leaned in closer to the door. He definitely wanted to hear the answer to this, even though he knew it.

At least...he thought he knew it.

"Yes and no," Søren said. "Neither of us are monogamous, if that's your question. But there's no subterfuge. Kingsley is practically married to a beautiful woman named Juliette who is his submissive. They have a daughter together, three years old and as precocious as her father. I have my Eleanor. She's also my property and *my* submissive. And also a masterful sadist herself. As is Kingsley."

"You're drawn to switches. Why is that?"

"I fell in love with both Kinglsey and Eleanor without knowing either of them were switches. It was never intentional. But I suppose if I were to put myself under Freudian analysis, you might say that I'm drawn to them because submitting is harder for them. It costs them."

"You're drawn to switches because it's hurts them more to submit to you? You really are a terrible man."

Søren chuckled. "They don't complain. Much. And it's 9:21."

"What do you prefer more? Men or women?"

"Women."

"Why so?"

"To paraphrase my Eleanor, 'Have you ever met men?'"

Kingsley's face hurt from trying not to laugh out loud.

"Ah, you are entertaining," Madame said. "Do you ever let Kingsley top you?"

"No. I'm a sadist. He's a masochist."

"That's not when I meant."

"You mean do I allow him to penetrate me?"

Kingsley winced. This conversation was getting personal fast. If Madame was going to ask intrusive personal questions, at the very least she could be nice enough to ask intrusive personal questions Kingsley didn't already know the answer to.

"That's my question, yes."

"No."

"Would you?"

"There was a time I considered it, but Kingsley never asked and I never mentioned it, either. And you know Kingsley...he's happy to be on the receiving end of both pleasure and pain. Both, preferably."

Both, *definitely*, Kingsley mouthed silently.

"Ah, very true," she said. "Your sadism interests me. How does it manifest?"

"Very simply, I get aroused when I inflict pain on a willing partner."

"How much pain?"

"Desires change from day to day, cravings. But always pain in one form or another. Pain that gives me power over someone. If you're looking for a formula, then simply this—the more pain I inflict, the more pleasure it gives me."

"Very dangerous math," she said. "Though I do sympathize. Have you any particular specialties or fetishes?"

Kingsley also knew the answer to that already. Blood.

"Cutting. Blood-play," Søren said. Kingsley awarded himself ten points. "I have a scalpel collection that surgeons would envy."

This was a fact. Kingsley had seen the scalpel

collection. And every year on Easter, Kingsley gave him one more to add to his arsenal.

"Cutting. Very good. You play often?"

"Not as often as I'd like. If only Kingsley and Eleanor could find a way to replenish their blood supply a little faster, I'd be a happier man. Until I was sent to prison for involuntary manslaughter, of course."

Kingsley smiled to himself.

"Do you ever enjoy receiving pain at all?" Madame asked.

"In certain contexts," he said. Kingsley's ears perked up. This could be very useful information. "Eleanor owns a set of metal talons, the sort that dominants put on their fingertips for scoring the skin."

"I know what they are."

"Sometimes she'll wear them when she's servicing me."

"You like being clawed at while she's sucking your cock?"

"It's quite pleasant, even when she breaks the skin. Especially then."

Kingsley did not need the picture in his head of Nora wearing sharp little talons on her fingers, blowing Søren and leaving bloody claw marks on his stomach, hips, and thighs.

Kingsley did not need that picture because Kingsley did not need to have an erection right now. He closed his eyes and thought of roomy Ford Explorers with dual-airbags, 401K retirement plans, Dockers, coffee from Starbucks, and ranch houses. It worked.

"And Kingsley? Has he ever inflicted pain on you?"

"He punched me in the face once, and the side. He broke a rib."

"During sex?"

Søren laughed and Kingsley grinned at the thought of punching Søren during sex.

"During a fight. I deserved it. He also deserved it when I repaid him in kind a few weeks later. All water under the bridge now."

"Is Kingsley the only man you've been sexually or romantically interested in?"

Long pause.

Kingsley stopped smiling.

"No, he's not the only man."

Kingsley's blood turned to ice.

"Who was the other?"

Kingsley's heart nearly burst from his chest.

"I spent some time in India in my twenties. When I was there, I met a young Sikh doctor. Jassa was his name. We became very good friends in my brief time there."

"He was handsome?"

"He was magnificent. Tall as I was, handsome, too. Very kind eyes. I'd never met anyone as compassionate as he was. When he tended a patient, he would thank them for letting him heal them. For someone like me who fetishes pain, it was a revelation being so close to someone who considered healing their life and their calling."

"Opposites attract?"

"Perhaps."

Kingsley died.

"Did you sleep with him?"

"No."

Kingsley was almost disappointed.

"He turned you down?"

"I never brought it up," Søren said. "He did, though, when we were discussing how colonization by the British Empire brought homophobia to India. Jassa believed that as the soul has no gender, same-sex relationships could be holy. I told him I found that a beautiful theology. He said something to the effect of continuing our 'theological discussion' later that night in his rooms, if I wanted."

"Did you want that?"

"I will admit to a fantasy or two."

"Really?"

"I was twenty-five, lonely, and he carried a sword."

"A sword?"

"A kirpan, a large dagger. It's an article of faith. I admit I might have had sword envy. They don't give swords to Catholics. Probably for the best."

Madame laughed softly.

"Not even one kiss?"

"I didn't say that."

Kingsley died again. Died and was resurrected. This was the most delicious secret he'd ever overheard in his life. What else was Søren keeping from him? They both needed to have a very long talk about what happened in their twenties when they were separated those ten years. Kingsley needed answers.

And photographs.

Charts and diagrams.

Home videos, preferably.

"You did kiss your Doctor?"

"I *might* have let him kiss me. It was the night before I was leaving India. We knew we'd never see each other again. Why not?"

"Did you enjoy it?"

"More than I expected to."

"But no sex? You don't seem a prude."

"I can't get aroused without inflicting pain. Jassa had given me no hints that he had any masochistic tendencies at all. Our respect for each other was as mutual as the attraction. I didn't want to lose his good opinion of me by telling him what I would have to tell him. Especially since he was a doctor. That's never an easy conversation for me, which is why I've had sex with so few people."

"How many?"

"I'm fifty-one years old and I've had intercourse with four people in my entire life. Kingsley had been with more girls than that by the time he was fourteen."

This was true. Kingsley would not deny it. Though it excited him more to hear about one clandestine kiss of Søren's than remembering all of his own high school conquests.

"Do you regret not sleeping with your friend?"

"No. But if I had, I wouldn't regret that either."

Madame laughed softly again.

"I've never told anyone about that kiss in my life," Søren said. "Not Eleanor nor Kingsley nor my confessor."

"Tell me this—who do you love more? Eleanor or Kingsley?"

Kingsley desperately wanted to know the answer to that.

And desperately didn't.

"Eleanor today, if only because she hasn't dragged me across the ocean to the bedside of a dying madwoman. Next week when Eleanor is making my life difficult, I'll love Kingsley more. I'm a terrible father, always playing favorites, and my favorite is the one who is annoying me the least at the moment. They are both well aware of this as I've told them in the hopes of improving their bad behavior. It hasn't."

That got a laugh out of Madame. And Kingsley, too, who laughed silently behind his hand. A very good answer.

"*Like a father playing favorites...* You see yourself as their father?" Madame asked.

"In a way, I suppose. Eleanor is fourteen years

younger than I am, so it's only natural we have that dynamic. Kingsley would say I created him. And he certainly acts up like a rebellious child sometimes."

"A prodigal son. Except you went back to him, didn't you? Not he to you."

"He left me," Søren said. "And I found him first. Eventually."

"How did you find him?"

"He was wounded in the line of duty and I was the next of kin listed on his medical forms. Someone in his agency called our old school and said that it was an emergency. I was contacted and told Kingsley's condition and whereabouts. I went to him then, immediately, but briefly. I'm still surprised he remembers that day. He was barely conscious. A year later we reunited in New York when I needed his help with something."

"If you didn't need his help...would you have gone back to him?"

A long pause. Too long. Kingsley wanted them to speak as fast as auctioneers. He wanted questions and answers and as many of them as possible.

"I don't know," Søren finally said. "Honest answer, I don't. After how badly things ended between us... I wasn't sure he would want me in his life. I am cruel and sadistic, I admit without shame or prevarication, but I'm not entirely remorseless. I'd failed him. I didn't wish to fail him again."

"And?"

"And..." Søren continued, a begrudging note in his tone. "He tempted me. Even after ten years apart, my desire for him was acute. I didn't trust myself to be with him. I didn't have enough self-control. He didn't have any boundaries or limits. If we'd become lovers again then, I thought I might kill him. I thought he might let me, the shape he was in emotionally."

"Self-destructive?"

"He was drinking heavily and using drugs, having unprotected sex with half of New York. In the early 90s at the height of the HIV epidemic. He's lucky to be alive."

Yes, Kingsley was very lucky to be alive. And he was only alive because Søren had come back to him at the right time.

"If we'd started sleeping together again then," Søren said, "it wouldn't have been healthy for either of us. The last thing he needed was another lover taking advantage of his craving for pain and self-destruction. I did offer to take him back, however, with conditions. He wouldn't accept my conditions."

"You offered to be with him again and he turned you down?"

"I required fidelity. He couldn't agree to that."

"Did you mean it or were you simply manipulating him?"

"I meant it. My life would have turned out very differently if he'd agreed. His too, I imagine.

And Eleanor's. Now I know it's for the best he turned down my offer, but it did hurt. And I did punish for that rejection by holding myself aloof from him for years. Though...I did give in one night a few years later."

"A good night?"

"One of those nights that comes to you when you least expect it and knocks the breath from your lungs. Yes, it was a good night. Eighteen years ago. It still leaves me reeling sometimes. And now it's 9:29."

Kingsley breathed through his hands. This was a mistake, hearing all this, hearing Søren's version of events that was so different from his own. He'd told himself that Søren didn't mean it when he offered to be with Kingsley again if he would be faithful to him. Was that why he said no? Kingsley's heart pounded. Madame was about to ask another question. Kingsley didn't want to hear it or the answer.

He couldn't stop listening.

"This will be my last question," Madame said. "And it will take all of our time, I think, for you to answer it."

"I'm intrigued."

"Kingsley told me a story about you and him, about a night you spent together when you were still school boys. You'd punished him by making him sleep on the floor. He remembered going to sleep on the floor but woke up in the bed with you. He told me this story because he wanted to know if I thought you'd picked him up in the night and carried him into your bed, like a child. He didn't think you, or any true sadist, could be capable of such tenderness. I agreed. But I think I lied to him. So that's my question to you. What *did* happen that night? Tell me everything. And don't pretend you don't remember. We both know you do."

Silence again. The clock was ticking and this time the clock was Kingsley's heart.

"I remember," Søren said.

"Go on then. Begin at the beginning. When does it begin?"

"That morning," Søren said.

"What happened that morning?"

"I'd received a letter from my father. A difficult letter."

"Why difficult?"

"My father was a sadist, too, the sort without a conscience. Even worse, he was incredibly wealthy, which made him one of the more dangerous men alive. I used to imagine my father kept a checklist of his favorite people to abuse and manipulate. He'd work his way down the list and then start over at the top. My name was at the top. And it was apparently my turn again."

"What did the letter say?"

"Demands, lies, manipulations, casual cruelties, threats. The usual."

"Any particular threats or cruelties you recall?"

"My half-sister Elizabeth was doing well, finally, at a new school. That my father mentioned it meant he was willing and able to use it as a weapon against me. If I didn't do as he asked, whatever he asked, my father would see to it that she was removed from that place and sent, like me, to a faraway boarding school, something I knew would destroy what little happiness she'd found. She'd told me many times I was the only person in the world she could trust. He taunted me about that, too."

Kingsley was astonished. He had no idea Søren's father had sent him letters at school, taunting and threatening him.

"You say your sister was finally doing well. What does that mean?"

"That is a Pandora's box you don't want to open, I promise you, Madame."

Kingsley was glad Søren put his foot down.

If Madame dared asked one more question about Søren's father or sister, Kingsley would stand up, open the door, say "We're leaving" and they would leave. No one, not even Kingsley, deserved a window into Søren's childhood. No one.

"Go on. The letter troubled you, as it would."

Kingsley breathed in relief.

"Before Kingsley, receiving a letter like that would haunt me for days. I would be ill, physically. Unable to sleep. I was unbearable company most of the time. After a letter from my father, I was dangerous company. Thank God for the woods outside our school. I'd retreat into them and run until I made myself sick. Or I'd walk for miles, barefoot if it was even slightly warm enough. It made me feel better when my feet would bleed. A release, in a way."

Behind the door, Kingsley rested his forehead on his knee. A wave of nausea, of sorrow, set him shuddering.

"Pain relieved the pressure, the feeling I might erupt or explode or..."

"Or?"

"Or walk until I reached a cliff and kept walking."

Kingsley's eyes burned.

"What stopped you?"

"My faith, such as it was."

"Your Catholic faith?"

"Yes."

"Are you still Catholic?"

"I am, yes."

"Devout?"

"Some might say that."

Kingsley nearly snorted aloud. Søren had a gift for understatement.

"You seem too intelligent to be beholden to such an archaic religion."

"Is that supposed to be a compliment?"

"Simply an observation."

"I see a painting and know there's a painter. God is the name we give to the force who painted the painter who painted the painting. I believe creation is good therefore the creator is good. No good apples ever fell from a poison tree."

"The world was an accident of random chance, atoms and molecules and trillions of years of things bumping into each other. A billion monkeys beating away at a billion typewriters. That's what I see. But you see artwork hanging on the walls and a Great Grand Being in a jaunty beret, merrily painting wars and rapes and famines."

"Kingsley was no accident of atoms."

"A work of art then, was he?"

"A masterpiece."

Kingsley looked up as if he could see the heavens from his hiding place on the floor of the bathroom.

"Besotted fool," she said. "I thought better of a fellow sadist."

"I might be insulted if you weren't lying in your dead husband's bed instead of your own, with a photograph of the two of you on your wedding day next to your pill bottles."

"Deep calls unto deep," she said. "I was talking about us both. Tell me the story. I want to know if I know you as well as I think I do."

"I received the letter from my father and as I did with all his letters, I burned it before anyone could find it and read it. Before Kingsley I would have risked burning it in one of the school fireplaces, but we had cleaned up the old hermitage to use for our trysts, if you want to call them that.

I took the letter there that evening to burn it. I hadn't asked Kingsley to come that night. The mood I was in, I didn't want to be near anyone. The letter was turning black in the fireplace when Kingsley opened the door."

Kingsley closed his eyes.

He remembered.

CHAPTER SIX

Kingsley opened the door and saw Søren standing in front of the fireplace. A fire was already up and burning.

"Thank fuck," Kingsley said. "It's freezing out there."

He strode over to the fireplace, past the rough wood table and chair, past the cot with the institutional plain white hospital-grade sheets and the threadbare patchwork square quilt, past the duffel bag on the floor that held their "supplies"—rope, a teacher's old telescoping pointer that made a brutal cane, and lubricant. A lot of it. Kingsley had stocked up before school had started.

He stood next to Søren at the fireplace and knew immediately he was in trouble. Six weeks into the fall term, Kingsley had figured it out. If Søren was in a good mood, he'd say all sorts of horrible awful things to Kingsley. Silence meant a bad mood.

And if Søren said anything nice or kind? Well, then he obviously had a brain tumor and needed immediate medical attention.

That evening he was silent.

"Uh, I saw you walk into the woods," Kingsley said. Søren had his suit jacket off, and his hands in his black suit trouser pockets, and his eyes were trained on the flames leaping off the hickory log on the iron grate. "Was I not supposed to come tonight?"

Kingsley tried to sound cool when he asked the question, like the answer didn't matter, like he wouldn't lose his fucking mind if Søren told him to go away.

"Doesn't matter," Søren said. His eyes remained trained on the fire. What did he see in those flames that Kingsley couldn't? He saw only the burning log, some ashes from the paper he'd used as kindling. He noticed then that Søren was barefoot and there was mud on his usually pristine feet.

Did Søren walk barefoot to the hermitage? Through the woods? In Maine in October when it was already dropping below freezing at night?

"You walked here barefoot?" Kingsley asked.

"Yes."

"Why?"

"Why do you care?"

"I don't know." Kingsley shrugged. "Seems like it would hurt, that's all."

"So?"

"So...I don't want you to be hurt."

Seemed obvious to Kingsley. Why wasn't it obvious to Søren?

∾

"*I ALMOST TOLD him about the letter right then, why I was hurting, why I'd hurt myself. The way he said it—'I don't want you to be hurt'... He sounded so young, and I felt so old.*"

∾

"MAKING THE FIRE'S MY JOB," Kingsley said. Joking. Teasing. Changing the subject.

"You weren't here." Søren's voice was flat, emotionless.

"I'm here now. So...should I stay? I mean, I don't care. You tell me."

Tell me to stay. Tell me to stay. Tell me to stay. Before St. Ignatius, Kingsley couldn't remember ever saying a prayer. Now he said them all the time. But not good prayers though. Not even prayers to God. Just prayers about Søren for Søren to Søren.

∾

"*I COULD TELL Kingsley didn't want me to make him leave. He was trying so hard to seem indifferent. Ter-*"

rible actor. Can't imagine how he ever survived as a spy."

"A good spy from what I heard. Mostly because he didn't really care if he lived or died. But with you, he cared. Harder to hide from the ones who know us, deep to deep."

"That's why I wanted him to leave. I was scared to tell him more about my father. He knew a little, and it was already too much."

"Did you tell him to leave then?"

"I wanted to. No, that's not true. I wanted to be strong enough to make him leave, but I wasn't. The mood I was in, I knew I'd say or do something to him that night I'd regret. For his sake, I told myself, make him leave. Make him leave before I told him what was in the letter, before I told him how sick and how...poisoned it made me feel."

"Poisoned? Such a strong word."

"There's a story we read my freshman year of high school—Rappaccini's Daughter, by Nathanial Hawthorne. Beatrice is raised in isolation by her father, a scientist who studies poison plants. She grows up in a poison garden, and as she grows, she becomes immune to the poison garden and yet poisonous herself. She cannot be kissed, because even her lips carry that poison. A man, Giovanni, falls in love with her and kisses her and he too becomes poisonous. He drinks the antidote which cures him...but it kills her. Giovanni was poisoned. Beatrice was herself...poison."

"You didn't want to poison Kingsley."

"There is no antidote for some poisons."

"But you didn't send him away."

"I was only eighteen. And who wants to be all alone in a poison garden?"

~

KINGSLEY STARED AT SØREN, waiting for the verdict. When it didn't come, Kingsley did what he always did when Søren gave him the silent treatment.

"Fine. Fuck it. Fuck you. I've got homework."

Sometimes that worked, telling Søren to fuck off. Not that evening. Kingsley grabbed his schoolbag off the floor and started for the door. He walked quickly, before Søren could notice how red Kingsley's eyes suddenly were...

"You can stay," Søren said as Kingsley reached the door. Kingsley turned to Søren. Søren turned to Kingsley. They faced each other across the faded wooden floor. "In fact, I insist on it."

Something in Søren's eyes, in the knife-edge to his tone...Kingsley almost wished he had been sent away.

He had a feeling this was going to be a rough night.

"I love you," Kingsley said.

Søren glanced up at the ceiling, in obvious and profound disgust. "Could you be any more pathetic?"

"I'm only saying it now because I think I'll hate you too much later to say it then."

Across the room they met eyes. Kingsley's back to the door. Søren's back to the fireplace mantel. What did Søren see when he looked at Kingsley? Kingsley would have given his left hand to know (the right hand, far more important). A nuisance? Probably. A toy? Definitely. A distraction? Maybe. A slave? His slave? Forever and ever and ever?

Hopefully.

What Kingsley saw was a blindingly beautiful monster. A shapeshifter. A solid rock wall by day when they had to pretend they were nothing to each other. A fire at night when they were alone together and were free to burn. Only a human after the fire was out when Kingsley knew it was safe to lay his head on Søren's stomach and the hand that ran through his hair wouldn't hurt him.

"I love you," Kingsley said again. This time out of sheer humiliating gratitude that Søren wanted him to stay.

"Come here." Søren pointed at the floor in front of him.

Kingsley dropped his bag again. He walked to Søren and stood where he'd been told to stand. His breathing turned shallow and his heart raced as Søren started to undress him. Jacket down the shoulders, down the arms, and onto the floor. Quick dexterous fingers made quick dexterous work of his stupid fucking school tie he was forced to wear. Also on the floor. With Søren occupied, Kingsley let himself stare. He stared at Søren's strangely dark eyelashes that framed the steel-colored eyes. And the too-perfect blond hair that glimmered like polished gold when it caught the sunlight between the trees. The mouth, also too perfect with the bottom lip just a little fuller than it needed to be for Kingsley to be able to concentrate on anything really, ever. And those lips slightly parted as if to invite a kiss. But Kingsley knew better to fall for that trap. He might lose his tongue.

And he needed his tongue.

Søren opened the top buttons on his shirt but stopped there. Kingsley tensed, waiting for the inevitable command. But there were no commands.

Søren kissed him.

For a split-second Kingsley was disoriented to be kissed like that, just kissed. Instinctively he knew it was a trick but he didn't care. He opened his mouth to the kiss, the pressure of the lips and the tongue on his tongue. Then he felt Søren's hand on the back of his neck, gripping him. And then Søren's other hand on his throat, pressing.

The kiss went on but as it deepened, so did the pressure of Søren's fingers on Kingsley's neck, the pressure of his palm on his larynx. The kiss started to hurt. Badly. Badly enough sounds escaped Kingsley's throat that, even to his own ears, reminded him of the whimpers of injured animals. How did Søren do that? Turn a kiss into cruelty? And why did Kingsley love it so much? Because it was so cruel? Or because, even cruel, it was still a kiss?

Kingsley grew light-headed. He could still breathe and that was the problem. He was near to hyperventilating from the intensity of the kiss. Dangerous as it was, he grabbed onto Søren's shirt, digging his fingers through the fabric and into Søren's sides.

Kingsley tasted blood and Søren must have tasted it, too. The kiss was so vicious, Kingsley had started bleeding. Hadn't he?

When Søren released his neck, Kingsley stumbled back a step. His mouth was swollen and ached. He stared at Søren who raised his hand to his bottom lip and wiped it with the back of his hand. The tiny smear of blood on Søren's lip disappeared. Then it came back, the droplet of blood. Gone. There again. Søren touched it with his fingers and then displayed the blood for Kingsley.

It hadn't been Kingsley's own blood he'd tasted.

Kingsley had bitten Søren.

"I didn't mean to. It was an accident."

Kingsley experienced all the symptoms of fear—the pounding heart, the sudden uptick in body temperature, tingling, dizziness. Even his apology sounded fearful. But he wasn't afraid.

Not really. Not yet. Exhilarated was more like it. What if Søren brutally punished him for biting him? What if Søren punished him more brutally than ever before...

Kingsley could only hope.

"Are you sorry?" Søren demanded.

"I am. I'm sorry."

Lungs burning. God, he really might faint.

"Beg forgiveness."

"I didn't mean to, I swear to God. I didn't even realize I did it. You were kissing me so hard, I think my teeth just sort of accidentally—"

"Beg on your knees."

Kingsley dropped to his knees onto the stone hearth of the fireplace. He didn't say anything. This wasn't the first time he'd been instructed to "beg" on his knees. Søren unbuckled his belt as Kingsley opened Søren's trousers. He took Søren's cock into his mouth, into his throat. And then he felt Søren's hands in his hair, holding him hard in place. He sucked and licked and rubbed and sucked again, deeper, harder, with abject devotion, like a penitent sinner kissing the feet of a saint's statue over and over again. And Søren must have been a saint of something. When Kingsley prayed for Søren to hurt him, Søren always answered that prayer.

The bare feet still bothered him, though. Søren's bare feet on the cold ground of a Maine forest in October. There was something Kingsley was missing, something not right. It seemed crazy to do that. It scared him...scared him like seeing someone who never drank alcohol suddenly downing a glass of whiskey or the well-dressed lady next door suddenly wearing rags. Knowing why Søren walked through the woods barefoot seemed more important than having sex. Usually there was nothing in the world more important to Kingsley than having sex.

But if Søren was hurting about something, maybe that was the thing that could possibly be more important than sex?

Kingsley pulled back and looked up at Søren. He expected to see Søren's head back in pleasure, or at least his eyes closed. But his eyes were open and staring, fixed on nothing. It was like trying to make love to a stone—hard but unfeeling.

"Are you all right?" Kingsley asked.

Søren started a little. Just a tiny bit. Just a flinching around the eyes. Søren looked down at him.

"Why did you stop?"

"I don't know. You just don't seem into this. You don't seem okay. I mean, what's with walking barefoot—"

"If I wanted to hear you talk, I wouldn't have put something in your mouth to shut you up. Do your job or leave. We aren't friends. If I wanted a friend, I wouldn't have hired a whore."

Søren said horrific things to him all the time.

All the time and every day almost. Most of it made Kingsley laugh. He knew it was Søren's way of flirting. But that crack about them not being friends, that made Kingsley's throat tighten up. Too tight. When he tried to get back to his "job" as Søren so tactfully called it, Kingsley couldn't do it. He tried and it hurt, and not the good type of hurt. Søren made a disgusted sound, half-sigh, half-growl, and Kingsley tried again, but he was miserable now, on the verge of tears which only Søren could do to him that easily.

"Useless." Søren put his toes against the center of Kingsley's chest and knocked him down onto his back.

And now Kingsley was mad.

"You don't like the way I do it, fucking do it to yourself then. You have your own head up your ass. I'm sure you can figure out how to suck your own cock, too. Christ, could you at least pretend to be human for five fucking minutes?"

Søren turned his back on him, straightened his clothes and simply said, "No. And if that's what you want, you should leave."

"So you did ask him to leave," Madame said.

"Finally."

"He didn't leave."

"He did, though. He did leave. And for the second time since I met him, I was scared he wouldn't come back. The first time I sent him a letter to order him back. What if that didn't work a second time?"

"I said it to him, and I will say it to you—you men are you own worst enemies."

"How many years did you sleep alone before forgiving your husband? Fifteen, was it?"

"Oh, shut up and tell the story."

◠

KINGSLEY DIDN'T LOVE SØREN. He realized that the second Søren turned his back on him and told him to leave. All that time, Kingsley had been deluding himself, thinking this was love he felt. He didn't love Søren. He just wanted to win this game they were playing. That's all it was, a game, and Kingsley kept playing because he thought if he played it well enough and hard enough and smart enough, he could uncover all the clues and put together all the puzzle pieces and the tumblers would turn and the dice would land double-sixes and he would win at last and the prize was, of course, Søren's complete and undying love.

And Kingsley was done playing. He was done because he would never win. So...fine. He would cut his losses. He would fold. He would never win, and he was a fool to keep trying. Dying old drunks in Vegas had better odds.

Kingsley came to his feet and pulled on his jacket and stuffed his school tie in his pocket, picked up his bag again and walked out.

Just...walked out, leaving Søren stretched out on their cot, reading his Bible.

There were things that needed saying, but Kingsley decided not to say them. He left without another word. More words would just throw good money after bad. All Kingsley allowed himself was one glance back as he walked out the door, one last look at Søren on their cot. With the door and the angle of entrance, Kingsley saw that the bottom of Søren's feet weren't just dirty from walking in the woods, they were bloody.

Not his problem.

Kingsley stormed away from the cabin but stopped at the edge of the clearing as if some kind of force field kept him from taking that first step into the woods and away from Søren for good.

The clearing around the cabin, it was almost a perfect circle. So perfect, in fact, Kingsley guessed it had been measured out by the old priests who'd put the hermitage here. Cabin at the center, bare ground it and a ring of rocks to keep the forest at bay.

When they'd finished cleaning and putting the cabin back together, Kingsley had made a joke, calling the clearing around the cabin their "fairy circle."

A gay joke, obviously, and Søren got it, but didn't laugh.

"Don't say things like that about us," Søren had said, sharply, coldly.

"Fuck, why not? Just a joke."

"I wouldn't let anyone call you that. Don't call yourself that. Or me. Either this—" and he pointed between the two of them, "is real or it's a joke. Decide right now which one it is."

"It's real," Kingsley said. And he hadn't made that joke again. It was a stupid joke anyway.

So Kingsley didn't step out of the clearing. Instead, he went to the old well with the cast iron pump that provided water from a deep ice-cold spring. Kingsley went to the pump and worked the rusting lever until fresh water flowed from the deep well into the bucket.

Water sloshed against his trousers as he carried the bucket back into the cabin. Søren turned his head as he walked back in and rested his Bible, open, across his chest.

"Are you going to throw cold water on me?" Søren asked, sounding bored.

"No, asshole. Cold as you are, fucker, you wouldn't even notice. Like throwing ice cubes at icebergs."

What Kingsley was going to do, and did, was wash the blood and mud off Søren's feet.

Kingsley set the bucket on the floor by the foot of the cot and dug a towel out of his rucksack. He'd learned the hard way to bring a towel with him to their nights together after a certain come-related incident in late September. Considering theirs was an all-boys school, Kingsley had a feeling the laundry service that took the dirty towels away just incinerated them all and brought back new towels every week.

He would rather be using the towel as a come-rag, as he usually did, but if he had to use it for the purpose God intended it, fine.

Fine.

Fucking fine.

"Sit up," Kingsley said.

Søren blinked at him. "Excuse me?"

"I don't want to get mud on the fucking quilt, okay? It's the only one we have. So sit up. I have to sleep there, too, and you're getting dirt on it."

"You scold like an old maid."

"I suck cock like one too, apparently. Sit up."

Was Kingsley actually doing this? Ordering Søren around? Apparently so. And the strangest part was, Søren did sit up. Kingsley saw a smile flit across Søren's mouth when he sat up, as if he were secretly amused by this sudden burst of suicidal behavior on Kingsley's part.

Whatever. Søren could laugh at his outburst all that blond fucker wanted.

Kingsley dunked the white towel into the water and quickly, and with zero regard for Søren's comfort, he scrubbed at the dirt and blood. The blood, Kingsley saw, was on the right foot only. A small cut that had bled profusely but would probably heal quickly. Well, it would heal quickly now that it wasn't caked with dirt. But just to be sure, Kingsley washed the wound again and dried it carefully.

~

"YOU'RE REMINDING me why I asked Kingsley to stay," Madame said. "Submissives like that are rare finds. Especially male submissives. To be that strong and that vulnerable all at once? I'll never forgive you for stealing him from me."

"He was mine first," Søren said. "I think the moment he washed the dirt off my feet was the moment I decided what I decided."

"And what did you decide?"

"That I'd find a way for us to stay together. No matter what it took."

"It meant that much to you? That Kingsley came to wash your feet?"

"No, it meant that much to me...simply that he came back."

~

"I'M FINE," Søren said, out of nowhere it seemed. Was he talking about the cut on his foot? Kingsley guessed so.

"If you get gangrene and your foot falls off, I will laugh at you. A lot." Kingsley washed his other foot and he wasn't gentle about it either. Not even when Søren put his hand in Kingsley's hair.

Kingsley ignored the hand and the thumb stroking his cheek.

"Leave me alone," Kingsley said. He didn't

mean a word of it, and Søren, of course, ignored the request.

"How does an old maid suck cock?" Søren asked.

Kingsley wouldn't smile. He refused to smile. But he really wanted to. And he really wanted to close his eyes and press his face into Søren's hand. The thumb on his cheek, right under his eyes, making tiny sensual circles...

"I don't know. I'd guess she wouldn't be good at it since she's never done it before? Or maybe she does it kind of enthusiastically?" Kingsley said. "Like, 'Hooray, there's finally a cock in my mouth! Just what I've always wanted.'"

"*Hooray*? Did you say *hooray*?"

"I guess she wouldn't *say* 'hooray.' Not with a cock in her mouth. But she would think it."

Søren's knuckles grazed the side of Kingsley's face. Then the hand was on Kingsley's chin and the thumb ran across his bottom lip. Kingsley's eyes fluttered in pleasure. Could someone come from having their lip touched? If anyone could, it was Kingsley.

"Is that what you think? Hooray?"

"When I'm sucking your cock?" Kingsley asked. He glanced up at Søren who nodded. "Usually I'm thinking 'Hope he doesn't get it in my eye again.'"

"That was your own fault." Søren tilted Kingsley's chin up an inch and leaned in. "Close your eyes next time, *Dummkopf*, or I'll make you stand in the corner again."

He had done that. Søren had literally made Kingsley stand in the corner for fifteen minutes as punishment after the Come Incident of Late September. And with no towel to wipe his eyes either. Lessons learned. Close his eyes. Bring towels.

"I don't know what's worse," Kingsley said. "Being called a dumb-ass or being called a dumb-ass in German."

"Close your eyes next time, and I'll be nice enough to insult you in French."

Kingsley did smile that time. A little smile, too small for Søren to see as Kingsley patted both feet dry. Then he tossed the towel into the corner of the cabin and looked up at Søren.

Kingsley was still on his knees. No reason to leave, not with Søren's hand still in his hair. And on his knees at Søren's feet was exactly where he wanted to be for all eternity.

"Take off your clothes and get into bed," Søren said.

Or that. Naked in bed was even better than being at Søren's feet for all eternity.

Kingsley stood up and undressed. To save Søren time, Kingsley went ahead and threw his own clothes on the floor, stepped on them a few times before pulling down the quilt and sheet and lying in bed, naked and hard and waiting.

Søren had undressed, too, and crawled into

bed on top of Kingsley. Then they were kissing again, like before. Søren's left hand gripping the back of Kingsley's neck, his right hand on the throat and pushing...the sounds, the whimpers of pain and need. Kingsley couldn't stop his hips from grinding up and against Søren. His cock ached, wanting to be touched and stroked and sucked. Was that another prayer? Must have been because Søren answered it.

Søren didn't suck cock like an old maid. Kingsley didn't think old maids would grip his wrists and dig their thumbs into the pressure spots there until his hands twisted in pain.

But it was heaven, lying there flat on his back, agony and ecstasy incarnate in the body of one teenage boy. His arms throbbed as Søren gripped his wrists tighter and tighter and Kingsley squirmed on the cot. The pleasure was intense, acute. Søren's mouth was as tight on him as the grip on his wrists. Kingsley found the side bars of the cot, pressed his heels down onto them and pushed himself into Søren's mouth. It was all he could do, trapped as he was by those vicious hands on his wrists.

His head fell back on the bed. His back arched. Kingsley tried to stay quiet, if only so Søren wouldn't know how much he was enjoying it. Always a risk. If Kingsley liked it too much, Søren might stop. But Kingsley couldn't stop groaning and panting and if anyone walked through the woods right now, they'd probably think he was being murdered. Maybe he was. Not that he cared. He couldn't think of a better way to die. He couldn't think of anything when the pressure increased on his wrists, on his cock. His testicles tightened and he cried out and at that cry, Søren released Kingsley's wrists. The combination of the release of pain with the rush of pleasure was blinding, obliterating.

Kingsley came and he came and he came. He came so hard his shoulders rose off the bed. He almost bent double from the sharp spasm of release that he felt in his cock, back, and stomach.

He fell back on the cot and lay there, eyes closed and panting, the muscles of his stomach still quivering deep inside. Limp as a rag doll, he put up no fight whatsoever as Søren took the ropes from their bag, stretched Kingsley's arms over his head, and tied his wrists to the bars of the cot. And though he felt the cold fluid on him and Søren's fingers, he was too spent to react to it. Not even when Søren's arm wrapped around his back to lift him did he say or a word or move a muscle. He was gone, a body without a will, and all that was left of him and in him was his total contentment to be used by Søren in any way that beautiful blond monster saw fit.

And Søren saw fit to fuck him.

The penetration was painless. Kingsley wouldn't have felt it if Søren came in his brain, he was so utterly gone. His entire body yielded to Søren. He moved only when Søren moved him.

Even the kisses on his mouth and neck and chest he barely felt, though he knew they happened and silently blessed the kissing god on top of him for each of those blessed kisses.

Søren kissed Kingsley from his collarbone to his ear.

"Do you really want me to be human?" Søren asked.

Kingsley shook his head no. "Never. Stay a god." Did he say that out loud or only think it? Didn't matter. Søren was a god and gods heard all prayers, spoken or silent.

Still limp, he didn't protest when Søren forced his legs wider and moved in even deeper. He could only stretch and groan when Søren's hand found his throat again and his mouth found Kingsley's mouth. This time Kingsley didn't bother watching Søren, waiting for him to come. Instead, he lay with his eyes closed, his back flat on the cot, and listened to Søren's tense breaths grow louder until they stopped a moment altogether as he finished inside him, filling him completely, all the way, until Kingsley could take no more.

How much time passed between when Søren pulled out of him and when he untied Kingsley's wrists from the cot? Who knew? Who cared? Kingsley only roused himself a little when Søren slid onto the cot with him again.

"Move," Søren ordered and Kingsley made himself move, but only to lay his head on Søren's stomach. Kingsley lay a long time in that halfway place between waking and sleeping, soothed by Søren's fingers running through his hair and occasionally tugging on it hard enough to almost hurt.

Almost. But it didn't hurt. Nothing did and nothing could. Not with Søren's stomach under his head and his come inside him. Since he was bulletproof and weatherproof and immortal, Kingsley pushed his luck, as he always did.

He asked, one more time, "Why did you walk barefoot in the woods?"

～

"LIKE A CHILD," Madame said. "They always know what the adults don't want to talk about, so they keep asking and asking and asking..."

"And asking," Søren said.

"What did you finally tell him?"

"I told him—"

～

"FLOOR," Søren said.

Kingsley lifted his head. "What?"

"Floor. Now. You're sleeping on the floor tonight."

"On the floor? Why?"

"One—because you talked back to me

tonight. Two—because I said so. Three—two is the only reason that matters."

Kingsley's jaw set into a hard line, and he didn't respond or even look at Søren as he got out of their cot. They only had the one quilt but spare clean sheets and luckily Søren didn't stop him when he grabbed a sheet from the pile, wrapped it around himself and curled up on the floor in front of the fireplace. His wadded-up clothes worked as a pillow, but not much of one.

The floor was miserably hard and cold even through the sheet. No way to get comfortable. Kingsley thought he'd never go to sleep, especially not with the thoughts running through his head. What had he done wrong? What had he said wrong? Or was this simply the price he had to pay for being in love with a god? Gods were cruel, weren't they? And arbitrary? Blessing you one minute, punishing you the next?

Or maybe it wasn't a punishment. Maybe it was a test. Gods did that, too. If it was a test, how would Kingsley pass it? He tried to think, tried to remember...what did the priests at their school say God commanded his people to do? There were the ten commandants, he knew that. But there was one commandant even more important than that.

Something Jesus said. Søren was big into Jesus. Big enough Kingsley occasionally paid attention in chapel when Jesus's name came up, which it did a lot at a Catholic school.

"*Master, which is the great commandment in the law?*" some disciple had asked.

And Jesus said something about...

"I love you," Kingsley said to Søren because the greatest commandment was love.

Søren laughed. A soft, cruel laugh.

"You said you'd hate me later."

"I didn't mean it. I still love you. And you can't make me not love you although you do a fucking great job trying."

"Go to sleep," Søren said. And since it was a commandment, Kingsley did.

~

"HE FELL *asleep on the cold hard floor. You bastard,*" Madame said. "*How cruel could you be? I almost want to shake your hand.*"

"*He told me he loved me. After the way I'd treated him that night...and right after he said he loved me, he fell sound asleep on the cold hard floor. And I lay there in the soft warm cot, wide awake and staring at the ceiling. I wanted him in bed with me so badly, it hurt worse than sleeping on the floor. I even wanted his head on my stomach again, where he always laid it when we slept together, God only knows why. Proof that love's a form of insanity. His head on my stomach is miserably uncomfortable. My Eleanor always sleeps on my chest, but Kingsley, it has to be the stomach, every time.*"

"You could have apologized to Kingsley, told him the truth, invited him into bed with you."

"Teenage boys can be intelligent, bright, accomplished, talented...but have you ever met one who was wise?"

"Ah, well, wisdom is the prize life rewards us for surviving our mistakes," Madame said. "You survived yours."

"Barely. I wouldn't mind a little less wisdom."

"No...neither would I. A little less wisdom and a few more nights with my husband. And you...a few more nights with Kingsley, his head on your stomach."

"I would happily make that trade, yes."

"So, tell me what happened next. Our time is almost over. Kingsley fell asleep on the floor. What did you do?"

"You know exactly what I did."

"Right off the floor? That couldn't have been easy."

"I was strong for my age, and Kingsley didn't weigh much at sixteen."

∾

KINGSLEY WOKE UP, and he was warm. Why was he warm? He lifted his head and saw he was stretched out on his side in the cot and his head was on Søren's stomach. They were in bed together. How the hell did that happen?

Søren was asleep. He could tell from Søren's steady breathing.

Kingsley must have woken up for a second, freezing, and gotten into the cot with Søren. If he got caught, he might end up sleeping on the floor for a week. Kingsley started to slide out of bed to get onto the floor again when Søren stirred. He stirred and wrapped his arm around Kingsley's shoulders, trapping him exactly where he wanted to be. Kingsley surrendered and fell back asleep in seconds. It was only when he woke up around 3 am, and Søren sent him back to school for the rest of the night...only when he was in his own bed in the dorm, did it occur to Kingsley...he didn't remember getting into the cot with Søren.

So how had it happened?

CHAPTER SEVEN

Now Kingsley knew.

"It's 9:55," Søren said to Madame. "Our time is up."

"Yes, I see that it is. And you've even given me the gift of one extra minute."

"With my compliments."

Kingsley detected the faintest note of sarcasm in Søren's tone.

"You gave me a gift and I'll return the favor. I asked you questions and you answered them. I'll now answer one of yours."

"There's nothing you know that I want to know."

"Do you want to know what he said about you when we'd drugged him?"

"No."

"Your self-restraint is admirable."

"If it's flattering, he's already told it to me in more ways that I can count. If it's insulting, then...same."

"You're being cruel to me now," she said. "I want to keep playing and you won't play along."

"I am cruel," Søren said. "Ask Kingsley. Ask Eleanor. I've cut them both open to the marrow of their souls, brutalized them both, physically, emotionally, and psychologically. And while you're at it, ask them why they let me. Now that's a question I would love answered."

Kingsley almost called out from his hiding place, "Because it makes her wet and my cock hard, *Dummkopf!*" but he refrained. Really, Kingsley thought, it wasn't rocket science. Why anyone would let Søren play with their mind and body and soul was hardly one of the great mysteries of the universe.

And supposedly Søren was the smart one.

"How is this then...I'll tell you why Kingsley sleeps with his head on your stomach."

"You can't possibly know that."

"I could make an educated guess."

"Go on then. If you need to tell me, I'm happy to listen."

Kingsley wanted to hear this, too.

Madame coughed again, that deep liquid wracking cough. But she recovered and began to speak.

"The last thing I said to my husband before I cast him out of the house was this—'You were supposed to protect me, and you didn't.' He promised that on our wedding night, that no matter what he did to me that was painful and seemingly cruel, he would always protect me. When I sent away all the male dominants and brought home only male submissives, then...finally...I felt protected. That's the beauty of a male submissive—they see women as their betters, their superiors. All the men who served under me were here for one reason and one reason alone—to protect the women of this house. Like guard dogs. Like knights."

"Like soldiers," Søren said. "Serving a general."

"No, like soldiers guarding a village of women and children," she said. "Which we were. The stomach is the weakest part of the body," Madame continued. "It's the most unprotected. A knife can be stopped by the thick bones of the sternum and ribcage. A knife to the belly is a death sentence. Kingsley sleeps on your stomach to protect you. When the knife comes down, it will have to go through him to get to your most vulnerable organs."

Søren said nothing to that at first. Kingsley had to give the old girl credit. Nail on the head.

"Game over," Madame said.

"Shall I fetch Kingsley now?" Søren asked.

"In the morning, I think. I'm too tired now. Much too tired. And I'd hate for him to see me like this."

"We'll come back in the morning then."

"No, no. Stay the night. We have rooms enough. Especially with the family away until

Friday. Ring the bell there. Colette will be up shortly to show you and Kingsley to your room."

"You're very gracious," Søren said.

The bell rang out loud and long and Kingsley came to his feet, wincing. He'd been sitting on a tile bathroom for almost an hour. When he heard footsteps outside in the hall, he snuck into Madame's pale blue bedroom. And when he was certain Colette was in Madame's room, he made a fast break for it. Down the hallway, back into the empty bedroom, back onto the balcony, down the drainpipe and in the window.

He made it back into the drawing room without getting caught. Once there he stood by the fireplace, straightened his clothes and ran a hand through his hair. Only then did he hear Colette and Søren approaching.

"Damn, I'm good," he said to himself. He might be an ex-spy but no denying...he still had it.

Colette opened the door and Søren came into the drawing room looking as if he'd spent the last hour having a pleasant cup of tea with a friendly old lady instead of having his soul raked over the coals.

"I'll show you to your room," Colette said. "This way?"

"We're staying the night?" Kingsley asked Søren, playing dumb.

"Apparently so. Madame said she'll see you in the morning."

"She will?"

"So she says," Søren said.

"If she's feeling up to it," Colette said. "Only then."

"Of course." Søren smiled at Kingsley the moment Colette turned her back on them. They followed her from the drawing room, up the stairs to the second floor and then through the heavy double doors.

"We're staying in the old wing of the house?" Kingsley asked.

"You're sleeping as far away from Madame as possible."

"How do you say, 'I am on Colette's shit list,' in French?" Søren asked in English, and Kingsley laughed.

"I speak English, too," Colette said, in English, of course.

"I assumed you did."

The corridor of the old wing didn't look much different from Kingsley's day. Maybe a fresh coat of paint. A few new old paintings on the wall. Colette took them to the room at the very end of the corridor, right before the door to the servants' stairwell. She took a key from her pocket and unlocked the door.

"I hope you'll both be very comfortable tonight." Colette waved her arm to usher them into the room. She flipped on the light switch and said, "Goodnight."

Then she shut the door behind them.

They stood in the room and it was a beautiful

room to stand in. Golden light emanated from a small crystal chandelier. A portrait of Madame as an exquisite young bride hung over the gas fireplace with an ornately carved mantel flanked with white taper candles in matching brass candlesticks. Bookcases lined the walls filled with French, German, and Italian classics bound in red, green, and blue leather. Matching armchairs sat on a plush Persian rug in front of the fireplace.

Only one small problem.

"No bed," Søren said.

"You know the château," Kingsley said.

Søren nodded. "Men sleep on the floor."

"I don't know what's more humiliating," Kingsley said. "That I didn't see it coming or that I'm actually enjoying this a little."

CHAPTER EIGHT

"This is my penance," Søren said. Kingsley saw him smile to himself.

"I'd say we sneak into another room, but..." Kingsley turned the knob on the door. Colette had locked them in. "We could leave through the window. Wait. No." Kinglsey patted his pockets. "She stole the car keys."

He'd left his jacket in the drawing-room while he'd been eavesdropping. Okay, so maybe he wasn't much of a spy anymore.

"We'll survive the night," Søren said. He seemed to be taking it all in stride.

"At least the fireplace works," Kingsley said, turning the knob and watching the fire spark and bloom. "Guess we'll camp out on the rug."

"I've slept in worse places."

"One question, though," Kingsley said.

"Yes?"

Kingsley asked, "When we're cuddling on the floor, can I be the big spoon?"

That question earned Kingsley the dirtiest look in the history of dirty looks. This particular dirty look should have been accompanied by the *Jaws* theme. Kingsley took that as his cue to say, "I'll find some blankets."

"Do that," Søren said.

Thankfully, the linen closet in the bathroom held sheets and blankets galore. And Søren found the liquor cabinet hidden inside an antique secretary desk. Kingsley laid the blankets out on the floor by the fireplace, turned the heat up, and took a glass of red.

Kingsley lifted it to his lips, then paused. "Are we sure it's not poisoned?"

"No," Søren said. He sat down on one of the chairs in front of the fireplace.

"You're waiting for me to drink first, aren't you?"

"Yes."

Kingsley raised his glass in a mocking toast. Before he could take a sip though, Søren drank his wine.

Kingsley lowered his glass, untasted.

Søren smiled. "I protect you, too."

Caught.

"You knew I was listening," Kingsley said.

Søren slowly nodded.

"You knew the whole time?"

Søren nodded slowly again.

"Can I ask about Doctor Jassa and his sword?"

Søren shook his head no. That didn't surprise Kingsley.

"Am I in trouble?"

Søren shook his head no again. That did surprise Kingsley.

"Really?"

"I knew you were there," Søren said. "I wanted you there. I would have been disappointed if you weren't there. Saves me from having repeat the entire conversation. Once was enough."

Kingsley laughed. "You didn't like Madame?"

"I have more than enough sadistic females in my life already. This trip was for you, not me. And I hope it was worth it." Søren took another sip of his wine.

"It was worth it when you told Madame you could leave, spend the night inside me and we'd forget her by morning. No, it was worth it in the drawing room watching you be a jealous bitch to Colette." Who was he kidding? "It was worth it when you agreed to come with me before we even left."

"I love you," Søren said.

Kingsley's brow furrowed. "That was unexpected."

"It was, wasn't it? I like to keep you on your toes. When I'm not keeping you on your knees."

"You're trying to get me into bed," Kingsley said. "Won't work. We don't have a bed."

"We can improvise. Drink your wine first while I decide what to do with you."

Kingsley raised his hand.

"Yes, Kingsley?" Søren spoke like a professor calling upon one of his students.

"Can I make a suggestion?"

Søren's right eyebrow inched upwards. If he smiled, Kingsley couldn't see it behind the wine glass.

"Go on."

Kingsley unbuttoned his shirt while Søren drank his wine. Kingsley dropped his shirt on the floor and then walked over it.

"Saves me a step," Søren said.

Kingsley went to the fireplace and removed the taper candle from the candlestick. He dipped the wick into the flame in the fireplace and presented it to Søren.

Before taking the candle from him, Søren met Kingsley's eyes.

"You'll like this, I promise," Kingsley said.

Søren set his wine glass onto the side table between the two arm chairs.

He took the candle from Kingsley.

Then Kingsley went down on his knees in front of Søren.

"I'm warming up to this idea," Søren said.

Kingsley said nothing. He only smiled as he started unbuttoning Søren's shirt. Button after button after button until it was all the way open and Kingsley couldn't stop himself from pressing his mouth to Søren's stomach.

"Again with the stomach," Søren said. But before Kingsley could explain himself, Søren let candlewax drip onto his back. With his head in Søren's lap, Kingsley's back presented an easy target.

Kingsley gasped and flinched when the wax hit but managed to take the pain without straightening up. He kissed Søren's stomach again, lower on his stomach, a longer, harder kiss... Søren dripped candlewax on Kingsley's back again. Another kiss, another drop of candlewax. One large dollop rolled down his back, burning all the way to the base of his spine. It scalded. It seared. It was delicious agony. And Søren seemed to be enjoying it as much as Kingsley.

Every time Søren let the wax drop, Kingsley kissed his stomach, or his ribcage, or his chest. Kingsley pressed his palm over Søren's erection, feeling it through his trousers.

Kingsley opened Søren's pants and took his cock into his mouth. Judging by how hard Søren's stomach contracted, that had been a good decision on Kingsley's part.

One hand held the candle but the other grasped Kingsley by the nape of the neck, fingers wrapped up in his hair. Søren inflicted the pain. Kingsley provided the pleasure. He sucked Søren long and deep into his throat, licked him and caressed him from the base to the tip with his tongue. He used his hands too, stroking the thick iron-hard length of him. On the dripping tip, Kingsley lavished warm wet kisses.

At no point did Kingsley try to rush things along. No, no rush at all. Kingsley was exactly where he belonged...on his knees with Søren's cock deep in his throat, white candlewax all over his back and the sound of his lover and his master's ragged breathing echoing in his ears.

Kingsley had the vague realization that Søren had blown the candle out and set it down. He dared to glance up once and his boldness was rewarded. Søren's head was back in pleasure, his lips parted, his throat exposed and his chest rising and falling. Kingsley memorized what he saw, burning it into his brain. It scalded like candlewax.

He bent his head again and returned to pleasuring Søren. Both of his lover's hands were now in Kingsley's hair, gripping him tightly, to the point of pain. Søren controlled the rhythm, the tempo, the depth. Kingsley let himself be used. Better to be servant of a god than a ruler of mortal men.

Kingsley prayed to his god that Søren wouldn't stop him. All he wanted was to swallow Søren's come. He wanted every drop of it.

Søren's thumb found Kingsley's cheekbone, caressed it and Kingsley glanced up one last time. He met Søren's eyes, dark now and hooded with desire. Kingsley had to force himself to look away. With all his love and lust and total devotion, he brought Søren to the edge of pleasure and they stayed there a moment together, locked together, sealed. Søren's stomach contracted again. Kingsley felt it under his palms. And when Kingsley dug his fingers into that vulnerable place Søren inhaled sharply and released.

Kingsley took every drop, every spurt and swallowed it like a starving beggar brought to a feast fit for a king. Only when Kingsley had emptied Søren out and drank his fill of the man did he lift his head.

Søren looked at him, lips still parted, panting. In the golden light from the fireplace, Søren glowed like a gilded icon.

Kingsley wiped his mouth with the back of his hand.

Then he said, "Hooray."

CHAPTER NINE

Afterward, they made use of the large old pedestal tub in the bathroom, a tub large enough for two grown men. Søren carefully cleaned the wax off Kingsley's back and washed the red wax burns with cold water.

"You think they're watching us?" Kingsley asked.

"The walls have eyes?"

"I had a bad habit of peeping through key-holes while here."

"Let them watch," Søren said, as he pulled Kingsley's back down against his chest.

After the bath, they dried off and laid down on the blankets Kingsley had spread over the rug. The fireplace provided the only light to the room.

Søren, of course, was the big spoon.

"Are you asleep?" Kingsley asked as a few minutes of silence passed without any sound but the wind outside the windows and Søren's soft breathing.

"Not yet."

"I'm sorry I eavesdropped."

"No, you aren't."

"All right, no. But I want to be sorry. How's that?"

Søren ran his fingers through Kingsley's hair. It was nice being naked and wrapped up in each other on the floor in front of a warm fire. Tomorrow morning when he woke stiff and sore, he might not find it so pleasant, but at the moment, Kingsley was more than content.

"I should have told you the things I told Madame before," Søren said.

Kingsley rolled onto his back, facing Søren. "You had your reasons for keeping your secrets."

Søren shrugged. "Bad reasons."

"We were young and stupid. And if you'd told me about your father...I wouldn't have known what to say or do. I know I would have made it worse for you."

"Maybe. Maybe not. Either way, I shouldn't have taken it out on you."

Søren meant that apology. Kingsley knew he meant it because he punctuated the sentence with a kiss, a deep and tender one, the kind of kiss that couldn't tell a lie.

"Forgiven," Kingsley said.

"And I forgive you for eavesdropping. Even though you can't seem to manage to apologize for it sincerely."

"I got to hear about you making out with a

doctor in India. How am I supposed to be sorry about that?"

"We weren't twelve-year-olds playing spin the bottle. We did not 'make out.'"

"But did you play doctor with him?"

"I need more wine," Søren said. "An entire bottle."

"Was there tongue?"

"Go to sleep, Kingsley."

"Was he a better kisser than I am?"

Kingsley gasped in extraordinary pain when Søren—without warning—yanked Kingsley's hair.

"Fuck..."

"Goodnight, Kingsley," Søren said.

Kingsley rubbed his scalp. "Goodnight, you absolute bastard. I love you almost as much as I hate you."

Søren rolled onto his back and, as he always did, Kingsley laid his head across Søren's stomach. Søren said nothing. For once.

"You aren't complaining?" Kingsley asked.

"There is a very good chance Colette will try to stab me in the night. Worth having your head compressing my diaphragm if it means she gets you instead of me."

"God, you're romantic."

"You have an erection. You can't be that offended."

"You've heard of hate-boners, yes? This is an offended erection."

"We're sleeping in front of a fireplace in a château library where you were briefly held captive by a mildly deranged sadist. What's not romantic about that?"

Søren asked a good question.

"It is pretty nice," Kingsley said, lifting his head to glance around the fire-lit room. "I mean this rug...This fucking rug is softer than a lot of beds I've slept on. Well, fucked on."

"How much do you think it's worth?" Søren asked.

Kingsley ran his hand over the Persian rug and felt the fineness of the fibers. The pattern was an intricate paisley, the colors black and gold. Truly unique, a masterpiece of weaving.

"More than most Americans make in a year," Kingsley said.

"Good."

"What?"

Søren rolled onto his side and pushed Kingsley onto his.

Then Søren grasped Kingsley's offended erection and stroked it.

Kingsley was not offended in the least by that.

"What the hell are you doing?" Kingsley asked. "Not complaining."

"I'm making you come. Now shut up and come."

"I'm not a dog. You can't order me...well, you can. But you should be a little nicer about it."

Søren put his mouth at Kingsley's ear and bit the earlobe...hard.

Kingsley took a ragged breath. "See?" he said. "That wasn't so hard."

While Søren nibbled Kingsley's ear, the stroking continued. Søren knew exactly how to touch Kingsley to bring him to the edge and leave him hanging there...and hanging...breathing hard and heavy...inching closer and pulling back...until the moment came—the tense, taut, tight, tortured moment right before...and then the final stroke, the bite on the back of the neck that would turn into a bruise by morning, and Kingsley came in almost painfully hard spurts.

He came all over the rug that had cost more than the average American made in a year.

Kingsley went limp. Søren leaned up and surveyed the damage.

"That's going to leave a stain," Søren said.

"Should I clean it off?"

"No."

"You're such a bitch." Kingsley had to laugh.

"They were cruel to you," Søren reminded him. "Only I get to do that. Now go to sleep before I put you to sleep."

Søren rolled onto his back and Kingsley turned over and lay across his stomach.

Kingsley sighed with contentment when Søren's hand found the back of his neck and caressed it gently with his fingertips.

"Søren?"

Kingsley's head rose and fell with Søren's utterly disgusted sigh.

"What now?"

"Can you believe this all started because you made me tell you a secret I'd never told you before. One order and we end up in France three months later."

"I will never *ever* play that game with you again," Søren said. "You have my solemn vow on that."

Søren closed his eyes. Kingsley couldn't quite sleep yet.

"Søren?"

"God, I hope that wine was poisoned." Søren sighed again. "Yes. What?"

"Tell me a secret you've never told me before..."

"I once killed a French whore in a château library."

Ah, well, it was worth a try.

Kingsley closed his eyes and willed himself to sleep.

"That letter my father sent me, the one I didn't tell you about... My father threatened you in it."

Kingsley raised his head, looked down at Søren.

"What?"

"Sometimes my father, when he remembered I existed, would call the school and demand a progress report from one of the priests. One of them, in his innocence, must have mentioned that I had finally made a good friend at school, that we were spending a lot of time together. The letter from my father told me I was required to apply to university immediately—Oxford or Cambridge were my only two choices—and/or get married as soon as possible. And if I put this newfound friendship with you over my education, my father would see to it you no longer were a 'distraction.'"

"That was a threat," Kingsley said. He knew a threat when he heard a threat. "Did he know we were together?"

"Not for certain. You're alive after all."

"You really think he would have killed me?"

Søren's father had been dead for twenty years and still Kingsley felt his blood turn cold as the grave.

"If he found out his only son and heir was sleeping with another boy? Let's put it this way— I have no doubt in my mind he would have used you to hurt me. To hurt and to manipulate me into doing anything and everything he wanted me to do. He used my mother and my sister to manipulate me. Why not you? When I decided to marry your sister, it was because I thought I was outmaneuvering him at last. I could get married, as ordered, and still be with you. And you would be safe. We would all be safe...finally."

But they hadn't been safe.

No one was ever really safe.

"Is that enough of a secret for you?" Søren asked.

Kingsley kissed the center of Søren's stomach again.

"That's enough."

He lay down again and the arm that wrapped around his back held him closer and tighter than Kingsley ever remembered it holding him.

"Sometimes I dreamed that we'd move to Paris," Søren said. "You and I. Attended the Sorbonne. Have a garret apartment with a four-poster I could tie you to every night. You weren't the only having fantasies of us running away together."

"I would have liked attending university with you," Kingsley said. "I can only imagine how you'd force me to do my homework."

"Unfortunately the Sorbonne doesn't offer a degree in Whoredom."

"Pity," Kingsley said. And then, "I love you, too."

"Go to sleep," Søren replied.

As ordered, Kingsley fell asleep.

CHAPTER TEN

Morning came early, too early, but a sharp knock on the door woke Kingsley with a start. Søren, used to rising early, was already up and dressed and reading.

"Good morning, sunshine," Søren said, closing his book.

"I hate you. Do we have any coffee?"

"I'll pour you a cup. But hurry. Someone's in a bad mood again this morning."

"Ten minutes," Colette said sharply through the door. "And then you'll leave. For good this time."

Kingsley dressed quickly, splashed water on his face, ran his fingers through his hair and swallowed his cup of coffee whole.

Ten minutes later, Colette came for them. Without a word, she ushered them into the hallway.

They followed her through the old wing and into the new, but instead of going to Madame's bedroom, she led them downstairs and out the front door.

"You're not going to let me see her, are you?" Kingsley asked Colette.

"You've already seen her," Colette said. "Don't pretend you weren't hiding in the bathroom. She knew."

"Yes, so did he." Kingsley pointed at Søren who only laughed. Colette did not like that laugh. She didn't like it at all.

"You think you're so superior," she said to Søren. "You have nothing on Madame. You have one little lapdog." Her chin jutted out, indicating Kingsley. "Madame has dozens. Men from all over the world will throw themselves on her grave when she passes. Madame is an icon, a legend. She's the Louvre. She's the Met. You're nothing but a child's drawing hung on a refrigerator. You are a shadow in her shadow."

Kingsley held his breath as Søren narrowed his eyes at Colette. This could get ugly, fast. Faces were about to get slapped. Hair was about to be pulled. Between a six-foot-four sadistic man and a righteously pissed-off French woman... Kingsley really didn't know who to put his money on.

"I'm sorry, I didn't hear you, Colette," Søren said. "Distracted by the mole on your chin. It really does look like a tick."

Colette took a step forward, murder in her eyes. Kingsley interposed himself between her and Søren.

"We're leaving. Right now," Kingsley said. "Let's go. Car's just outside the gate. Colette, *adieu*."

"Your car is being brought round," Colette said. "I look forward to watching you drive off in it."

In the faint gray light of the early spring morning, Kingsley saw their car easing down the drive toward the house. The car pulled up in front of them and the door opened.

Madame stepped out, dressed in an elegant black suit with a crisp white blouse underneath. She looked hardly a decade older than when he last saw her.

And she certainly didn't look like she was dying.

Kingsley stared at her. Søren stared at her.

From behind them, Colette laughed.

"*Adieu*," Colette said.

"Your keys, gentlemen," Madame said. She handed them to Kingsley, who did and said nothing when Madame kissed him briskly on each cheek. She smelled of lavender water and looked exquisite, healthy, beautiful. "*Adieu*." She kissed Søren on each cheek as well. "*Adieu*."

Madame followed Colette into the house. The door closed behind them.

"I don't know what's more humiliating," Søren said. "That I didn't see that coming..."

"... or that you enjoyed it?"

Søren laughed. Ah, Kingsley did love that laugh.

"She fakes dying very well," Søren said as they walked to their car. "That cough of hers sounded tubercular."

"I thought she was dying, too, I swear."

"When she touched my face, she was running a fever. I felt it."

"Easy to fake," Kingsley said. "Hot water bottle under the sheets."

"And the pill bottles with her name on them? Those were narcotics."

"Her husband's? She could have changed the labels."

"Makes perfect sense."

"Don't feel bad. She was literally married to a spymaster, and she fooled him for years."

"I don't feel bad at all. Only amused."

"You know Colette is laughing at us right now."

"I'm sure she is," Søren said. "I don't mind. Let her laugh all she wants. At the end of the day, one of us has a tick on their face and the other doesn't."

"You don't think it's cute?"

Søren looked at him, eyebrow cocked.

"Drive," Søren said. "Take me to Paris."

They got into the car and drove away.

"Madame beat us," Kingsley said. "She won."

"I wouldn't say that."

"Well, we did leave the giant come stain on her rug."

"I was thinking of the note I left in the room on the fireplace mantel."

"Wait, what did the note say?"

"It said I lied to her last night. One lie only."

"One lie? You lied to Madame? About what? Kissing Doctor Jassa? Lifting me into bed? Nora's blowjob talons? What? What did you lie about?"

"She'll never know." Søren looked at him. "And neither will you."

"Motherfucker," Kingsley said.

"I anticipate that will be her response as well. Or the nearest French equivalent."

"You're really not going to tell me what lie you told her last night?"

"I'll give you a choice. I'll either tell you what the lie is or...I'll fuck you tonight until you forget you ever saw that château."

"You would have to literally fuck my brains out to make me forget the château. You would have to do unconscionable things to me. I would have to be broken. *Laws* would have to be broken. God would be offended by what you'd have to do to me. Fuck, *Satan* would be offended."

"Yes, and that's exactly what I'm offering. I'll tell you my lie. *Or* I do such things to you to make the devil clutch his pearls. What will it be?"

Kingsley turned from the château drive onto the forest road and headed west to Gay Paris.

"This is so unfair. You are an inhuman monster," Kingsley said. "A bastard of the highest order. I don't know how you live with yourself sometimes. Can you please be human for five fucking minutes?"

Søren turned his head and smiled at Kingsley, the sort of smile that made the car windshield steam up.

"What's your answer?"

Kingsley wanted to say, "Tell me what you lied about." He did. He wanted to. He really and truly and desperately wanted to be the sort of man who had the self-control and the self-restraint and the dignity to pick the secret over the sex.

But facts were facts.

Two plus two was four and Kingsley Edge was a whore.

"Fuck me," Kingsley said. "But I'm not going to like it."

He was going to like it. He was really going to like it.

"I thought that's what you'd say."

"But if I find out you were lying about getting kissed by your magnificent Sikh doctor, I will *never* forgive you. You'll be dead to me. I won't ever let you fuck me again."

"Ever?"

"Ever," Kingsley said. "At least six months."

A few minutes passed in silence as they sped along the autoroute.

"Do you want me to be human?" Søren asked him. "Really?"

Did Kingsley?

Did he really?

Nø.

FIN

ABOUT THE AUTHOR

 Tiffany Reisz is the *USA Today* bestselling author of the Romance Writers of America RITA®-winning Original Sinners series from Harlequin's Mira Books.

Her erotic fantasy *The Red*—self-published under the banner 8th Circle Press—was named an NPR Best Book of the Year and a Goodreads Best Romance of the Month.

Tiffany lives in Kentucky with her husband, author Andrew Shaffer, and two cats. The cats are not writers.

Subscribe to the Tiffany Reisz email newsletter and receive a free copy of Something Nice, *a standalone ebook novella set in Reisz's Original Sinners universe:*

www.tiffanyreisz.com/mailing-list

Tiffany Reisz's *USA Today* bestselling Original Sinners series returns with the long-awaited sequel to *The Queen*.

The Priest is the beginning of a new era for Reisz's Original Sinners series, and the perfect jumping-on point for new readers.

eBook, Paperback, and Audio from
8th Circle Press and Tantor Audio

This signed-and-numbered hardcover edition of *The Chateau* is limited to 500 copies. Includes the bonus novella "The Story of Ø" (aka "The Return"), as well as exclusive alternate cover artwork on the dust jacket.

"Masterly and rich.... Highly recommended."
— *Library Journal* (Starred Review)

8th Circle Press Signed & Numbered Hardcover
Available Exclusively at TiffanyReisz.com

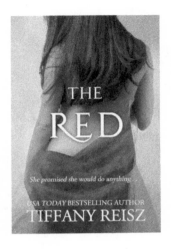

Mona Lisa St. James made a deathbed promise that she would do anything to save her mother's art gallery. Just as she realizes she has no choice but to sell it, a mysterious man offers to save The Red...but only if she agrees to submit to him for the period of one year.

"Deliciously deviant.... Akin to Anne Rice's 'Beauty' series." — *Library Journal* (Starred Review)

eBook, Paperback, Library Hardcover, and Audio from 8th Circle Press and Tantor Audio

Return to *USA Today* bestseller Tiffany Reisz's Original Sinners series with *Winter Tales*.

This collection includes three fan-favorite Tiffany Reisz Christmas novellas, plus a brand-new novella *(December Wine)* exclusive to this anthology.

eBook, Paperback, Library Hardcover, and Audio from 8th Circle Press and Tantor Audio